Stranger In The Fire

ISBN: 9798990729308 (paperback)
ISBN: 9798990729315 (ebook)

Names: Corvidae, Cornelius, author.
Title: Stranger In The Fire / Cornelius Corvidae
Description: New York: Rare Bird Publishing, 2024

Cover art by Cornelius Corvidae.

Printed by Rare Bird Publishing in the United States of America.
First printing edition 2024.

Rare Bird Publishing
An imprint of Secretariat Communications LLC
secretariatcommunications.com

Stranger In The Fire

Cornelius Corvidae

Contents

From behind my eyes stretches a shadow showing darkly.
From within my throat crawls a deathly rattle rasping lightly.
Outward both are drawn into the world to trace a truth less brightly;
Outward both, so as to dampen the sun's most blinding glare
With a woeful shade of the soul's most darkening despair.
Alas, I'm gifted with a world to be witnessed without fear;
Alas, a world too dark to see the demons dancing near.

Chapter 1

There are waves of wind drifting across a hilly landscape, impressing quietly their shape into miles of moonlit field. The air is damp and cold. The grass of the field is long and gray. Apart from the quiet tumbling wind, all is silent.

Standing among the hills is a solitary silhouetted tree with branches like black skeletal fingers, and beneath their upward grasp—in their darkest shadows—a boy sits resting.

He sits cross-legged with his back against the bark. His eyes are locked in a deep gaze upon a house that stands a stretch of field away.

The house is average and presumably belongs to a family—a husband and wife, with a child or two. Large and two-storied, it stands with white-painted walls that glow softly under the yellow, slivered moon. Save for a nearby barn that is decrepit and crumbling with age, it is the only building visible for miles.

A long unpaved driveway along the house is overgrown by

wild grass and hardly visible. It runs to a road more public somewhere behind the hilly horizon.

Since the set of dusk the boy has watched the house with eyes tireless and patient as ancient stone. He has watched for signs of life and taken notice that no cars are present and no light but the moon or stars has shone since his arrival. He has concluded that the house is unattended for the night.

The boy rises. There is a shakiness in his legs and for a few moments he flails his arms excitedly and kicks his legs about; he jumps up and down, trying to calm his nerves.

He stills himself and stiffens his legs and then looks upward at the dark of heaven; the darkness dotted infinitely by galaxies of fire and gas. His breath slows and the night air fills deeply into his lungs.

A slow exhalation, and then excitement surges through him. He picks up the gas can he brought with him and begins walking toward the house.

His pale white face looks disembodied as he moves across the landscape. His clothes are darker than the night—and his hair is black to match—so he is a ghosted head floating through the darkness. All the while his blood is pulsing wickedly within him. He stretches his free hand outward and reaches gently into the tall swaying grass as he walks.

The smell in the air is damp and sweet; cut grass. The yard around the house and barn has been recently tended to. As he nears the tall white house his eyes fix upon the aged and tattered barn. Its roof looks to be moments from caving in. Its walls are ancient and paintless, almost worn to dust. He walks intently toward it.

The large front entryway doors hang open and are creaking back and forth in the pulsing breeze; deep darkness lies within the barn, and the boy walks into it without hesitation. Inside, his blood warms in the fear and the not-knowing of all that lies hidden in the lightless silence.

The only sounds are his breathing and the swaying doors behind him. He turns and walks out from the darkened belly of the barn.

He begins circling the perimeter, all the while wetting the barn's outer walls with splashes of gasoline, his arms rocking back and forth like those of some farm-field reaper. When he finishes relieving the last of the gasoline from its can he walks to the house and sits upon the small stoop of steps at its doorway.

A fog has crept across the fields and he sits secluded in its smoky veil. Each breath he lets out becomes calmer and softer than the last. He lets out a quiet whisper, asking, "Isn't it beautiful?" His words come out vapor and then dissolve in the cold air, with no one to answer to them but the silent voice of God.

He rises and walks back to the barn. From his pocket he pulls a book of matches. He tears one loose and strikes it into flame. It breathes warmth onto his hands and the familiar smell of sulfur tickles his nostrils. He throws it down and the gasoline-wet wall ignites.

The flames are quick to grow and with a whoosh they unfold from nothingness, wrapping like a heated hug around the barn's entirety. The wood begins to crackle, and with the crackling comes a sound that is like the low-pitch torrent of flapping wind—the deep tumbling breath of fire.

He closes his eyes and imagines a river of flowing, molten lava deep beneath the surface of the earth, yearning to erupt. He opens his eyes and stares blankly at the orange-light incandescence lapping at the building before him.

As the flames take their hold more deeply into the barn, he steps back from the brilliant light and hissing heat, and then there is a rustling from within the barn's upper level. A large flock of small, shadowy birds flutter out from the upper window opening.

"You should thank me," he says aloud. "I've set you free."

His eyes stare contentedly into the fire's warm orange light. Soon the barn's roof buckles and crashes down, sending a cloud of sparks and embers spraying into the air. The boy's eyes are empty black holes, unfazed and hardly blinking as they witness the gold and red fiery flakes raining through the darkness.

Chapter 2

The boy sits lone upon a wood bench. A mid-day's graying sky is showing through a windowed ceiling high above him. Various stores and their onlookers surround him. The air is thick with echoed voices.

The boy sits still as a statue in the midst of all the mall people's erratic meanderings. He watches the strange world before him with a strange intentness all his own. When one passerby does chance upon a meeting of their eyes with his, they find themselves discomforted by the seeming lack of life behind his stare and they are quick to search for something else to feign interest in.

Near where the boy is sitting is a store stocked with various housewares, and in its window hangs an ancient-looking clock from which a golden pendulum is ticking slowly back and forth. The boy's eyes break from their weighted gaze and drift lazily toward it. He takes note of the time and stands and smoothes the creases of his attire and begins walking.

He is a spectacle among the sea of blundering, trend-dressed people. His black suit is perfectly fitted upon him and his steps are fluid and graceful, as if his body contains no weight or presence in this world. He glides by on the outskirts of the awareness of others, unnoticed as a shadow or a ghost.

Lingering like a cloud of smoke in the air around him are multitudes of pained and hungered voices. Tinny children-cries bound outward from the innards of every store. No doubt all of them deprived of some toy that is the world's worth entire within their crying eyes. And circulating nearer is the collective whine of teenagers, all berating their parents for not having bought them the latest in technical gadgetry. And the parents. All explaining why they cannot afford such things.

He slips through the crowds, disinterested, walking until he comes upon a small, almost-hidden store at the end of one of the mall's long halls. The unsightly store is situated between an enormous department store and a pet store where encaged animals can be seen fighting amongst themselves.

He stops and stands and watches silently over the store for a moment, as if to make certain it is the correct place for him to be. He then steals a glance at the wristwatch of a passing person. After confirming the time he continues purposefully toward the store.

Upon the store's entryway door is a crudely hand-painted

sign. The words *Uruboros Books* are scrawled upon it. Each of the words is made up of colorfully painted snakes formed into letters, with each letter feeding upon the letter that succeeds it, save for the final letter in the line; the final snake the only one allowed an open mouth, starved for sake of having nothing to feed upon. The boy smiles and whispers quietly to himself, saying, "That is the snake to be."

The store's lighting is soft and yellow like a candle's glow. Behind the front counter a male employee whose face is red with acne sits reading. He's not interested enough in the boy's entrance to look up from his book. His nametag reads *Brad*.

The boy glides past him. He walks toward the store's end, peering down each book aisle as he passes. The store appears entirely empty of customers, until he is near the back of the store and begins to hear voices.

He walks to the aisle nearest them and stands listening, blocked from view of the people speaking by a shelf of books.

"You are not yourself, Cathedra. This is not you. Can you see yourself?"

It is the gentle voice of an older man. The voice of a young girl responds meekly to it.

"Richard. I'm scared. You keep saying that. But if I'm not me, then who am I?"

"All that I'm asking is that you look at yourself. Do you see what you're wearing?"

The girl's voice ages suddenly, becoming defensive and cold in tone.

"So, I'm just supposed to be whoever you say? Huh? Is that it? Shall I put on a sweet little dress, get dolled up, and find a man to work his life away for me? Perhaps you want that man to be you? Is that it, Richard?"

"Cathedra, I need you to calm down."

"Do you want to fuck me?" The girl lets out a forced laugh. "You're quite the catch, aren't you? You manipulative pervert. Is that what you do when you've a creature under your care? You try to fuck it?"

"Is that what you believe? That you are just a 'creature' to me? And I am only trying to fuck you?"

There is quiet and then a breathy sigh from the girl.

"Cathedra?"

"Richard... Oh, poor Richard... lost his wife and child... thinks he can save them through me... poor, poor Richard."

"Shut up," the man growls at her. "Shut the fuck up."

"Oh... so in control, aren't you, Richard."

"I... You... Why do you do this? What do you want from me?"

"Nothing. You are pathetic."

The man exhales a slow and controlled breath. "I can't help you if you don't want my help." The man is moving, his voice drifting in the air. Soon the boy sees him passing by his aisle, talking as he does. "I will be at my office—awaiting your next breakdown."

He finishes his sentence as a whisper, his words meant only for himself. The man's voice does not suit his appearance, as he looks much younger than he sounds. He is dressed in a wrinkled white dress shirt and tight-fitting faded jeans. Pale brown hair which is neatly combed and parted from his face hangs nearly to his shoulders. As he passes from view the boy takes note that the man's hair is an absolute mess at the back of his head, tangled and knotted like that of a feral human.

The man's footsteps carry off softly as he exits the store.

Moments pass by without so much as a movement or a sound from the girl, and the boy leans out from behind the bookshelf to see her idly facing a wall of books with her back toward him. She is crying.

The girl senses she is being watched and turns, revealing a young but firm face, gaunt and pale as moon and framed by short and wavy blonde hair which has been styled by whatever surface the girl most recently slept upon. Her eyes are a deep hypnotic blue. Her cheeks are wet with tears. "Don't worry. You've got nothing to offer," she says.

"Excuse me?"

"Yes I'm hurting, and no, you've got nothing that could ever help so please fuck off."

"I don't want to help you. I'm only watching. Who was that

man?"

"A man tasked with looking out for me. He's kind, in the most selfish of ways, and he's got a scar I like to poke at when he becomes... tiresome."

"And who are you?"

"I..." She takes a moment to consider. "I am someone who's becoming bored of you and your questions."

She smiles wickedly and then she begins whimpering; a quiet, pained moan leaks out of her which she quickly forms into a loud, guttural wailing. It is the pitiful sound of a child attempting to draw attention to their feigned sadness. All the while her eyes are calm and coherent, staring into the boy, awaiting a response. The boy simply stares back, unfazed.

It is not long before the store's employee comes upon them. "Sir. Er, miss. Are you okay? Miss?"

The girl becomes silent and she glares coldly at the boy. The boy watches her as a raven would, curious and undaunted by her efforts to scare him off.

"Yes. I'm just delightfully wonderful," the girl says bluntly, although her eyes tell a different story. "And if you'll excuse me, I'll be leaving you two gentlemen."

She walks past the employee, who has a very confused look on his face. The boy follows after her, into the hall beyond the store, and into the dense crowds of people. She walks faster, trying to lose him, often looking back to see, disappointedly, that he is still close behind her.

When she reaches the mall's glass entryway doors she stops as she's putting her hands upon one of the handles. She freezes for a moment then looks to the boy who is standing beside her.

"Jesus. What the fuck do you want from me?"

"Nothing. And I'm not Jesus, I'm Radey."

"Are you going to keep following me?"

"Yes. I think I will."

"You're strange, very strange."

"So I've been told."

Outside, the parking lot is dull and gray beneath a sky that is the same. The girl walks across the lot and the boy follows suit. She walks to a solitary patch of grass near the parking lot's edge and she sits beside a small tree, within the shade of it. The boy stands watching over her. Above them is a soupy murk of slowchurning storm clouds.

The girl removes her shoes and socks. She presses her bare feet into the grass. She seems to be relaxing. "I don't like being stuck inside," she says. "Gives me anxiety."

Directly in front of the two of them a car pulls into an empty parking space. The car's two front doors click open in succession. A man and a woman step out in unison. Both of them close their doors and then begin walking toward the mall's entrance. They don't notice Radey and the girl, and they don't notice they are being watched by them.

The man is dressed in a dark red-striped sweater with dull brown corduroy pants. The woman is dressed in a slick long-cut dress, colored darkly with grays and blacks. She looks like she is going to a funeral, while the man looks like he could be on his way to teach a kindergarten class.

The man and woman don't make it far from their car before the woman stomps one of her thick-heeled shoes against the ground loudly as if to make a point. She stands still like a pouting child. She is throwing some sort of silent tantrum, awaiting a response from the man. He stops and turns to her.

"Honey. We can't keep doing this," he says. "Every time it's the same. You say that things are fine and you are okay and then we come all the way down here and you refuse to go in."

Again the woman stamps her foot onto the ground.

"No. I can't do it, I can't do it, I can't do it."

"Yes, you can, honey. Yes you can. There's nothing behind those doors that you can't handle."

"I'm scared. My heart is beating so fast, I can hardly breathe. I want to go home, now. I need to go home."

"There is nothing to be afraid of, I promise you. Trust me, the world behind those doors is the same as the world we're standing in right now, and I'm with you either way."

The woman stands shaking her head back and forth, her face pale. She turns and walks back to their car and gets into it.

The man stands waiting where she'd left him with a pained look on his face. It is not long before he gives up, defeated. He walks slowly to the car and gets into it.

The two of them are vaguely visible behind the reflection of gray sky in their car's front window. Drops of rain begin to sprinkle on the glass and soon the two of them are hidden entirely from view by water cascading down the windshield.

Radey and the girl watch the car in silence. Then Radey speaks.

"Witness the end game of a love traced out in fear and comfort."

The girl giggles softly and says, "They don't look very comfortable."

"It is an incessant desire for comfort in a world where they deserve none that has led them here—to this apparent cycle of panic and defeat. To be free of it they must each let go of the other. They are clinging to that which imprisons them: fear."

"Fear of what?"

"Death. Without it we are free beings in this world."

"Without fear of death, we become exactly *that*... dead."

"Beyond life there is nothing; death is not a thing and there will be no thing to experience it. To fear something that does not exist is a delusion not worth entertaining."

"So why don't you just end your life?"

"Life *is* death."

They each are quiet for a spell, listening to the falling rain. Then the girl asks, "So Radey, your strangeness, is it a blessing or a curse?"

"I am only strange in the eyes of others. I'm no stranger to myself. *That* would be a curse. For example—" He points his finger like a grim reaper's claw toward the car that the couple is still sitting within. As if on cue, the engine starts and the headlights come on. The car sits humming, with its lights brightly shining upon Radey and the girl for a few moments before it drives off. "They run from their true nature; they flock like cowards before the turning of the sun. Then wonder why they wake in lifeless darkness."

"Yeah... maybe. Are you clever? Or just vague and insane."

"What do you think?"

A stroke of lightning splits the sky with a forked line of blinding white. The sky flashes purple for a heartbeat.

"I don't know yet." The girl studies him for a moment, then says, "I'm going to do something I will probably regret."

"What's that?"

"I'm going to tell you I want to see you again. And by the way, I'm Cathedra. But I suppose you already knew that."

The sky shivers with a low rumble of passing thunder.

"Yes," he says solemnly.

Chapter 3

Radey's footsteps carry through the darkness. The light fixture is broken but he walks with sure-footing for he has walked these steps many times before. His feet knock softly down the wooden steps until he reaches their end and steps onto smooth concrete. He begins walking with his hand outreached until it touches upon the cold steel of a door. He pushes it open and cold air flows over him, and with it the scent of formaldehyde.

He enters into the unlit room, which is dead silent. He stands for a few moments simply breathing his gentle breaths amidst the blackness. It is a thick blackness, not unlike the sort a panicked prey would find itself in after being swallowed by a predator. He ponders such a thought for a moment before saying aloud, "And God said, let there be light."

He runs his hand across the wall to his right. He finds the room's lightswitch and flicks it on and a momentary shock of blinding brightness fills his vision. His eyes adjust, and what comes to be is the sight of the room he's come to do his job in.

The room is almost entirely white save for the shiny silver of various tools and cabinets. At the center of the room a white porcelain table sits like some sacrificial altar. Lying atop it is a lumpy mound blanketed in white sheeting. Radey glides past the mysterious pedestal to the sink at the room's end where he washes his hands vigorously.

After drying his hands he retrieves a white paper gown from a nearby cabinet and fits it onto himself. He moves to the porcelain table and pulls back the veil of thin white fabric. Beneath it is the naked corpse of a woman. Lifeless and gray, she lived perhaps sixty or seventy years before death came to claim what life had loaned her.

The skin of her body is translucent and yellowing slightly, with an intricate mess of meandering blue veins webbing throughout, their chaotic pattern visible beneath that which was once her way of feeling the world outside her but is no longer.

Radey scans her body like an insect sizing up its prey. Her frame is small and frail. Her abdomen is swollen with fluids. There are patches of purple bruising blotched across the entirety of her form. Greased and wiry white hair frames her leathered face. Her eyes are closed in such a gentle way it is as if she is only resting.

From beneath the table he retrieves a spray bottle and begins spraying her body with it. The smell of disinfectant becomes a thick cloud in the air and seeps burning into his nostrils. After dousing her completely in the stuff he sets the bottle down and then he sets his hands upon her body. He begins massaging her arms, moving them each up and down, like the levers of some contraption he's controlling. And then her legs, each one massaged and loosened from its stiffness.

Once he has finished relieving the rigor mortis from each of her dead limbs he walks to the door and opens it. He stands holding the door open and clenching his breath while he listens for any signs of life beyond the stairwell.

All is silent in the upper levels of the building and so he goes back to the porcelain table. He removes his white paper gown and lets it drop to the floor. He stands before the lifeless woman as a black-suited silhouette in the room of white and silence.

He moves to the head of the table and places his hands on the sides of her face. He moves his fingers so as to touch her closed eyes with the bare skin of his thumbs; the feel of her eyelids is like that of wilting flower petals. He pushes them open to reveal the milky orbs beneath. Within them cradled is the emptiness of death; the tranquil glassy stare peers into him, and he into it.

"Death; my mother," he whispers. "Make my eyes as your eyes are, so I may see the world for what it is."

Chapter 4

I want to gouge my eyes. The lifeless, loveless colors of this room are a hindrance to my soul; the barren beige walls, carpet the color of puke. Every piece of furniture is brown and bland and horrid in its plainness.

There is nothing further from God and nature than the lighting of this room; intentionally dull and gentle—the unthreatening glow meant to make me feel comfortable while he probes the world within my skull.

Richard sits across from me. His pale brown hair has grown long and his face is specked with stubble. He's wearing a dark brown sweatshirt and jeans. He does not look like a therapist or anyone you'd pay to be in the presence of. He wants his patients to see he's average; that he's not overly concerned with appearances.

"Cathedra. You seem a bit ill at ease. How are you feeling today?"

Oh, Richard. I get it. You want me to know how much you

care. You want me to believe this is only casual conversation so I will let my guard down and let you see the various ways that I am broken. But I won't, because you already know everything about me, and every word you speak is a trap. A badly disguised trap set to catch anyone stupid enough to pay you for their entrapment. You are a snake too fat to hide in grass and if I were honest I'd tell you that you make me want to strangle something.

"I don't know. I guess... confused, I guess." The voice that comes out is not my own. It is weak and frail, afraid. Oh, Richard, so wonderful the effect you have on me.

"It may help to lie down—to get comfortable," he says, calmly.

He is pinching a pencil in his hand. He has a pad of paper on his lap, but he never writes anything.

"Okay."

I lie down. I rest my head on the arm of the couch. I stare up at the blankness of the ceiling. I breathe deep. I still want to choke someone.

"Have you thought about our last meeting? At the bookstore?"

"Yeah. What about it?"

"What was it that upset you?"

I turn my head to face him. I think: It was your hollowed heart. It was your impotence and fear. You're chasing ghosts to exorcise your own past. You are a selfish, hopeless man, only interested in absolving yourself of your own pain. I think: I want to hurt you.

"Please, Richard. Do we have to talk about that?"

"No. What would you like to talk about?"

"I don't know."

"How's your job?"

My head throbs. "It's fine. Same old stuff. How's yours?" I laugh and I don't know why.

"Cathedra, you're not really giving me much to work with, here. More importantly, you're not really giving yourself much to work with."

"I'm sorry but—"

"Cathedra, can we talk about your parents for a second?"

He's trying to catch me off guard, and he's succeeded. He knows just the words to turn mind into a house of shattered mirrors and churning shadows. Thousands of tiny, prickly spider legs are tickling like wildfire across my nerves, burrowing their way toward my insides. I think I feel sadness. The couch begins to feel warmer and softer beneath me. My blood feels lighter and the room begins moving as if it is afloat; a ship at sea.

"I can't do this." My voice squeaks out like a pathetic wounded mouse. My heart is hammering at my chest. The couch is turning into quicksand and I stand up to avoid passing out and sinking into a sleep from which I'd surely never wake.

"Cathedra. It's okay. Calm down, it's okay."

I look at him. I want to hate him but I can't. My hatred is gone. Instead I blurt out, "No. Nope. Can't do this right now. I need fresh air."

I walk fast from the room and leave him sitting in his chair. I run for my car. I get in and drive toward the opposite end of the universe.

Chapter 5

The sky is an electric, cloudless blue above me. I'm miles from town and Richard is only a memory and I'm feeling better knowing he hasn't the faintest knowledge of where I am, and neither do I.

Soaring over roads unnamed and scarce of cars, I ride the cracked and faded pavement into the further unknown. The roads take me as a river would; I flow upon their path free of worry or concern—through forests thick with young spring growth; through fields tall with gold, swaying grass; through hilly fields alive with bright green colors.

The sun is hanging as high as I feel, and I'm set on driving until it sets to darkness.

The hours blur, and as the golden light of the late afternoon begins to show over the horizon behind me, I come across a sight unwelcome to the countryside. Jutting from the dark green of the forested horizon ahead are enormous geometric shapes. Arcs and loops, as tall as buildings, winding through the sky as silhouettes amidst the boundless blue behind them.

I wonder for a moment if I've happened upon a top secret government facility, meant to be hidden amidst the hours of nature I've driven through to get here. I consider slowing the car and turning around, but think better of it.

As I draw nearer to the mysterious monuments, I begin to make out the details of their architecture. Each loop and spiral and arc is made of intricate lattices of wood and steel support beams, and there are tracks laid upon them. And careening upon the tracks are carts full with people, their arms all waving about in a collective panicked fit, or perhaps in celebratory joy.

Roller coasters of every sort soar through air in every which way above the treeline. Never in my life have I visited such a place—a place designed purely for pleasure and release—and what better time than now to do so?

I spend the evening riding the park's rides. I wind and corkscrew through the sky. I shoot like a rocket toward the sun. I get tossed and turned while buckled within a small cage. I get strapped in and spun dizzy in a compartment that looks like an apple from the outside. I drive a miniature car fitted with a soft bumper on all sides, for ramming into other people in cars suited the same.

Lastly I find myself floating down a meandering river of crystal-clear blue water. The plastic vessel that is my vehicle is painted brown and made to look like wood from the outside; a hollowed-out log cast down an artificial river.

The cartoonish vessel meanders mechanically through bends in the rushing water, guided by an unseen rail connected to the underside. After a succession of turns it takes me into a darkened concrete tunnel made to look like a mountain on the outside. When I emerge from the concrete cave I'm lifted slowly to the peak of a steep slope, after which I come crashing down and splashing through the waters on the opposite side.

It is in this moment—the moment of water rising up and raining down on me—that I feel bliss, simply and truly. Time slows and the world hangs, lit golden by the sinking twilight sun; the crystallized droplets of water glisten around me like teardrops in a snow globe, fleeting and beautiful for their ephemerality.

The wetness soaks through my clothes and touches cold upon my skin; a baptism if I've ever had one. I should come here all the time, I think to myself.

I roll on through the water to the ride's end. A big, dumb smile on my face. The ride attendant comes and helps me out from the hollowed tree-trunk. He is young and dressed in loose clothing and his face is wet with sweat and streaked with dark stains of an origin I'd probably rather not know.

"The exit's over there." He points my way to an open gate that leads out of the park, letting a thick scent of body odor waft out from under his lifted arm as he does so.

The day's light is waning and the park must be closing, and I'm ready to go home anyway.

As I'm walking toward my car and crossing the long parking lot, I see something of a startling coincidence. At the parking lot's end, where the pavement ends and the forest begins, I see the boy in the black suit from the mall. He is leaning casually against the trunk of a large tree, watching me. I approach him slowly, second-guessing whether or not it is really him.

"What are you doing here?" I call out to him.

He pushes off the tree without a word and begins walking into the woods. I call out to him again but he doesn't hear me, or acts as if he doesn't. I walk to the forest's edge and then stop. He stops also, seemingly in response to me having stopped. He turns to face me.

He speaks out in a jumble of worded nonsense, loudly, as if it bears significant meaning to him.

"Time is not the veil we walk upon; it is the light lifted from the empty beast; brought up from the mind and body collided with the spatial void; heated whilst in the final tides of suffering; drank like poison till we slip the boundless death upon our chests; into it we shed our selves like a snake would shed its skin." His eyes are rolled into his head, the pupil-less whites of them staring back at me. It gives me the creeps.

"What the fuck are you talking about? How did you know I

was here? Are you following me?" I call out to him but he doesn't respond. I begin to walk toward him and he once again turns his back to me and leads me further into the forest.

I follow him until I can hardly see the parking lot. Dusk is setting in and the light is graying darkly and soon I may not be able to find my way back if I keep following him. I give up. And the moment I stop walking he turns to face me, as if expecting me to change my mind and follow him further. "Fucking weirdo," I whisper aloud.

I turn and head for my car. I'd look back to see if he is following me but I am feeling infuriated with him and don't want to give him another second of my attention. Why the fuck was I following him in the first place, I think to myself; am I really so careless? He is clearly insane and for all I know he wants to lure me away from civilization and kill me. Jesus. Now I'm feeling scared and panicked and I'm half expecting him to wrap his arms around me suddenly and drag me screaming into the darkness. I walk faster, and then I begin to run. The air is nearly black with night and the trees slap me with their branches all the way back to the parking lot.

When I get to my car I look back but see no sign of him. I get in my car and begin driving home, feeling awful. Welling up inside me is a dark and boundless sadness, as if someone has died and it's all my fault.

I was carefree for a few fleeting moments today. Peace

swept in and kissed my heart so gently and beautifully, and then it vanished just as fast as it arrived and it may as well have never appeared at all.

Happiness: You can go fuck yourself; you are a fragile eggshell poised to crack at the lightest touch; you're full with rotting poison and darkness, set to taint anyone foolish enough to hold you in their hands.

Actually, scratch that. Radey. *You* can go fuck yourself. I blame you for this. I was fine until you showed up.

Oh God. Was he stalking me? How else would he have known where I was. What if he's following me right now.

I check my rearview mirror and see only darkness and I can't help but feel like he is out there, pursuing me.

Chapter 6

A white orb bleeds soft light into an otherwise pitch-black night sky. The yard light stands amongst the mowed green grass of Richard's front lawn.

The Doppler yawn of distant cars joins the wind as it whispers softly through the leaves of darkened trees, which sounds like a gentle hiss of coursing water in a stream. Richard's house is deeply secluded with forest on every side.

At the edge of the house's backyard, amidst the brush and blackness, Radey sits crouching.

Within the house Richard is pacing back and forth in view of Radey. He is preparing a meal and is visible through the largest of his house's windows. He appears oddly content for someone living alone; upon his face is a fragile happiness, the sort reserved for persons unaware of all the wonders and worries that exist beyond themselves and the world they've grown accustomed to.

Radey watches as Richard eats a meal and then cleans up after himself and afterward moves out of view and into another room. Radey moves as well, never losing sight of him for more than a few moments.

Richard spends the final waking moments of his night sitting at a desk and typing on a laptop within a small study. When he leaves the room to go to bed, Radey remains outside the window, where he waits well into the night.

Once he's certain Richard must be deep in sleep, Radey moves closer to the house—close enough to see his breath fog the glass of the study window.

He pushes open the window and crawls into Richard's home. He glides silent as an apparition toward the desk Richard had been sitting at. He fingers through its drawers and finds a mishmash of sundries and office supplies and, much to his luck, a pad of paper with perhaps every password Richard has ever used scrawled upon it.

He logs into the computer and searches its files until he finds a folder named *Cathedra*. Within it he finds a long list of dated folders, each with typed documents stored inside. He copies the contents of the folders onto a USB drive and then he places the device into the pocket of his suit and leaves the room, entering the hallway.

He peers into each of the darkened rooms as he passes them. The entire house looks professionally-cleaned and hardly lived in, like the interior of an office building. There are no paintings. No televisions. Only practical items and furniture. He peers into a bedroom at the house's end and finds Richard sleeping soundly in his bed, alone and unaware of the waking world and all its malevolent churnings.

Radey turns from the room, leaving Richard to his mind's lonely dreamings. He moves into the unlit kitchen at the hallway's opposite end, where he stands and stares in the dark at an old photograph. The picture is stuck by a magnet to the refrigerator. Upon it, frozen in time, are the smiling faces of Richard and a woman and a child.

After a long while staring at the photo, Radey lets out a gentle whisper. "Oh, Richard. The things you'll never save... and the things that will never save you. Tonight you'll meet them both."

He reaches to a nearby spool of paper towels that are hanging from beneath a cupboard and he unwinds the spool entirely, creating a mound of the stuff upon the floor. Near him is a stovetop, and so he lifts the heap and places it messily upon the stovetop's burners. Behind the stovetop is a window and from it he gently unhinges some curtained drapery to lay it atop the mountain of paper towelling.

He dials all the burners to their maximum temperatures and stands watch until the paper towels erupt in silent flames. The kitchen brightens quickly in the small fire's incandescent orange glow. The flames reach and waver upward, licking at an overhanging assemblage of white-painted wooden cupboards.

They begin to char and turn to blackness in color. The wood will soon catch fire.

Radey goes back to the study and exits through the window, leaving the house to turn to ash with Richard still inside it.

Chapter 7

A muted night sky yawns overhead. Drifting slowly through it are gray clouds glazed orange by the glow of the city which holds my home. I've been driving for hours.

It is 3 a.m. and I am dreading what may await me within my house when I return to it. I can only hope my father is passed out drunk and that he hasn't even noticed my having been gone for the night.

I pull onto the block where my house resides. The neighborhood is dead and quiet and lit obscenely bright by streetlights; their light is an attack upon my senses. I can't help but feel the light itself is somehow conscious of me—that it is watching me, and judging me. I can't help but feel something terrible has happened, or is going to happen. I breathe deep and try to calm my heart. Such is the feeling of dread which always seems to accompany my returning home.

I drive past rows and rows of doppelganger houses, each one a duplicate of the others; white rectangular boxes all, each filled with the same appliances and furniture and people with their dreams long dead and beyond resuscitation. This is my neighborhood. This is my home. This is where my mind was molded.

A cold sweat wets my skin as I turn the car from the main road and onto the driveway beside my house. I park and sit and stare at the sad white box in which I live—which matches identically to all the other boxes of the neighborhood. Sadness uncoils inside me, like a den of nested snakes waking within my heart, all coming to their senses to scatter and spread like poison through my veins.

This must be what a domesticated bird feels like as it's returned to the confinement of its cage after being given a brief taste of freedom.

What keeps me coming back to this house—the thing that *owns* me—is my mother. I love her more than a wing loves wind, and I always will. If it weren't for her, I would have flown this horrid coop ages ago.

All of the lights within the house are turned off and this, at least, sets my mind at ease. It means my mom and dad are sleeping.

When I get inside the house I breathe in the cold dead air of the unlit living room, and then I let it out. I watch the expelled vapor of my lungs swirl and turn to nothing in the darkness. The kitchen ahead of me smells of alcohol. I close the front door behind me as quietly as I can and then I begin to tiptoe across the living room floor.

As I'm drawing careful steps across the carpet toward the hall that leads to my room, I hear something; a quiet shuffle in the darkness. I freeze. The house is lifeless and silent, but a ghost is watching me. I can feel it.

A deep, forced exhalation sounds from behind me and my heartbeats become solid chunks inching up my throat. I can't breathe.

"Where were you?" The voice is deep and cracked and raspy, spoken from the mouth of either a demon or a lifelong smoker.

I turn to look at him; he's in the dark somewhere and my eyes are struggling to adjust. The floor creaks as he takes a step toward me from somewhere in the shadows.

"I'm sorry, Dad—" I choke out each word. My legs are trembling and I still can't see him. "I got lost and it took forever to find my way back and... I'm sorry, I didn't mean to be gone so long."

"You would leave me to worry all night about you?" His voice is getting closer and it's not long before I can make out the soft blur of his silhouette. He staggers toward me drunkenly. "How can I sleep without knowing if you are okay?"

His question seems so innocent and is posed so quietly, nearly a whisper, but I know his voice well enough to feel the anger seething beneath his words.

"How can I rest when you could very well be dead?" His words are growing louder, the anger brimming more clearly from his throat with each successive syllable. "You are all I have in this horrible world. Do you not care how much your actions cause me pain?"

His facial features are formless in the darkness, and his head is shifting oddly from side to side as he speaks; his movements are those a zombie might make. For a moment I imagine him moaning the word *brains* as he stumbles toward me.

"I'm sorry, Dad. I'm so sorry." I feel the heat of tears running down my cheeks.

He stops when he is close enough I could reach out and touch him. He glares silently at me, as if he's trying to will some sort of punishment into me telepathically, and it's working. My eyes have adjusted well enough that I can see the rat's nest of short black hair draped messily over his wrinkled, pale face. His eyes are shadowed black almonds in the darkness—the eyes of an entity more alien than any other I've ever met.

"I'm sorry. I'm sor—" My world goes dark in the middle of my sentence, darker than dark, and I hear a sound like popping meat. A breathless squeak rushes from my lungs.

I'm laid out on the carpeted floor and when I realize what has happened my hands are in a panicked fit, touching upon my face, both of them covered in a warmth that is streaming from my nose. He hit me and knocked me clean off my feet, and there is blood gushing out of me, lots of it.

I would cry out but who would I be crying to? He is standing over me, staring down at me like I am trash and I'm expecting him to hit me or stomp on me, or kill me. He shakes his head in disgust and walks past me. He walks from the living room, down the hall and into his room. Some part of me can't help but wish he had, in fact, killed me.

This is my home. This is where my mind was molded.

I get up and go to the kitchen. I run cold water at the sink, which makes a tinny sound as it runs from the faucet onto the mountain of empty cans and bottles beneath. I splash the freezing water repeatedly onto my face but the bleeding doesn't stop. I decide I don't care and I walk bleeding to my bedroom at the end of the hall, next to my parents' room. I go to bed with my face throbbing and my pillow soaked in the stuff that keeps me here.

Chapter 8

Dry air sweeps my lungs. I wake to a bedroom dully lit by a newly risen sun. My face is stuck to my pillow and I have to peel the fabric of the pillow case from my cheek. The house is silent. I rise from bed and stumble to the living room, hoping dearly that my father is gone.

I find my mother sitting idly within her wheelchair, where my father must have left her. She's a statue, staring out the living room window like some product of human taxidermy, only breathing. She's been this way for years and I guess I should be grateful as it's a miracle she's still alive. I walk to her and wipe the drool off her chin. I kiss the top of her head and say, "I'm sorry."

Long blonde hair frames her face, waved and with a mind all its own; it's much like mine, only longer. Her skin is free of wrinkles and seemingly untouched by time, as if her condition has stopped her aging.

"Will you ever wake?" I ask of the air and as I do tears run warmly down my cheeks.

I stare into the irises of her eyes, still beaming brightly the color of ocean, each of them. What lingers behind those eyes? I wonder.

I stand beside her for a long while with my hand upon her shoulder. I'm waiting for her to move, to show some sign of life. It never happens and you'd think it would get easier, but every day it's harder and today my heart feels like it may collapse from the weight of it. If there were a God I'd wish for him to be trapped in this moment forever, as punishment for all the atrocities allowed under his watch.

"Do it, God... snap your fingers. Do a magic trick and make it all go away. Do something. Help me."

I trace my mother's stare to the world outside the living room window, but all I see is the palely reflected image of myself. Dark dried blood all across my face. I look like a zombie. Worse, actually; zombies at least are free from the experience of debilitating sadness, and I'm about the saddest sight I've ever seen.

I hate to admit it, I really do, but I need Richard. He is all that stands between myself and total depression, or insanity, or... something even worse; I don't want to find out what.

I go to the kitchen and dial him on the phone. I get a receptionist whose politeness aggravates me.

"Hello. You've reached the offices of Schwartzbach and Richardson, how can I help you today?"

"I need to speak to Richard."

"Oh, I'm sorry, dear. Richard didn't come in today."

"I really need to talk to him... can't you call him, or something?"

"I have not been able to reach him, trust me, I've been trying."

"But... how can he do this? What use is he if I can't even get a hold of him when I need him."

"If this is an emergency, Dr. Schwartzbach is available to all of Richard's patients. Would you like me to connect you to Dr. Schwartzbach?"

"No. I need Richard. Put Richard on the fucking phone."

"I'm sorry miss, but you don't need to take that tone with me. He is not available and swearing is not going to change that. Now if you'd like, I can—"

I hang up before I swear at her again.

"God damn it. God damn it."

Panic sets loose on me like a pack of feral dogs; there are bat wings aflutter in my lungs, and my heart is an over-filled helium balloon, and my thoughts are a faint mist that hardly qualifies as any sort of coherent thing.

I begin to worry about what will become of me if I can never reach Richard again, and what will happen when my father comes home. I worry about death and what will happen when it comes to claim me. I worry that I may be dying now, or that I may already be dead.

I need to numb myself, and fast, before my mind unravels completely and I become some worthless trembling thing upon the floor. What I decide to do is cut myself.

I can think of nothing better than physical pain to dispel my mind's imaginary torment—torment that becomes more real the longer it's allowed to linger. I go to the kitchen. I open the cutlery drawer near the kitchen sink. As I'm fingering through the steel spoons and forks, searching for a sharp blade, I hear a voice.

"You don't need to do that, and you don't need Richard. Not anymore."

The sound startles me so much I think my heart may have actually burst. A knife slips from my fingers and I turn around to see Radey sitting in a chair beside the living room window, opposite my mother. He is looking at her and shaking his head.

"You're not real," I say.

"I'm as real as you are."

"That's... comforting."

He shifts his gaze from my mother to look at me. His stare is deep and penetrating.

"You have a darkness in you—a darkness which Richard never knew what to do with."

"There's never been anyone else willing to help me. No one but him."

"I can help you."

"But, before... at the bookstore, you said you didn't want to help me."

"You said you didn't want me to. I will help you if that's what you want. Is that what you want?"

I look to my mother. My eyes water and I have to look away. I look to the spot of blood on the floor from the night prior. I look behind me to the open drawer where I'd just had my hand upon a knife. A tear runs down my cheek and I quickly wipe it away.

"I don't know what I want." My voice comes out in a familiar squeaky tone which I hate dearly.

I look to my mother once more and say, "I want you to help me."

"Are you sure?"

"Yes."

He stands up and goes to the front door and opens it. He stands there waiting, looking at me. "Come with me," he says.

"What about my mom?"

"She'll be fine. Trust me."

He walks out the front door, and I follow in his steps.

Chapter 9

*Months earlier; an entry from Richard's private
journal, stolen from his computer.*

"My heart is a volcano," Cathedra spoke to me from across
a small table. We were waiting for a waiter to return with the food
we ordered. Cathedra's hair was an uncombed mess—her face
mostly hidden behind it. A room of cleanly dressed patrons were
eating and talking all around us.

"It fills my veins with black ash and dread instead of blood
and love," she continued. "I just... I just don't know how to not
look back. Like Lot's wife. You know, from the Bible."

The tabletop between us was made of white marble,
charred with pale streaks of black and shined to the point of
being reflective. I caught myself watching her mirrored face in the
stone instead of looking at her directly.

"I saw something a long time ago that I wasn't supposed to
see, and all I have to do is not look back... but I just can't fucking
help it."

"How do you know you weren't supposed to see what you
saw?" I asked.

"Because it made me what I am, and I don't want to be what I am. Nobody should have to see—"

Cathedra's voice was drowned out by the sound of dozens of plates and other tableware items as they were knocked to the floor by a clumsy server. The young waitress apologized frantically in the wake of her accidentally created chaos.

"Oh my God, everyone. I am so, so sorry."

The other patrons were quieted. Cathedra, however, was unfazed and hardly gave the server a second thought. "I'm so weak," she said. "The foundation of my self is made from the dust of death. The lightest breeze can pull me apart and take me away. And I welcome it to do so."

I felt the weight of more eyes than hers upon me. The quiet in the room had not yet faded and she'd been the only person speaking in those last few moments. Our conversation had become of public interest and for it I didn't know how to respond to her.

She continued, oblivious or uncaring of the attention she'd gathered. "What is this feeling in me? Haunting each moment. Stealing the light from me. Life once was filled with the breath of beauty, and then one day it became infected; it no longer lights with love and happiness. It's been hollowed out, rotted deep into its core."

And then she became quiet, her eyes scanning lazily the world outside the restaurant's window. It was raining. The street was busy with cars and people.

The other patrons had lost interest in us and were back to discussing more pressing matters—like what they'd witnessed the night prior on television, or what style of clothing they considered to be most fashionable.

"And when did this happen? When did life first feel that it had become infected?" I asked.

"My despair begins and ends with my parents. They are my inescapable tragedy. I am their ghost, doomed to haunt them." Her voice was trailing off, like her words were suddenly a secret to be kept from all those around us. "Does it even matter? Is it really the type of thing that can be cured?"

"Yes," I answered. "It does. And yes. It can. And none of this is inescapable. We can find a way out for you."

She swallowed hard. She didn't believe me. Not even slightly.

"I can't even dream of happiness anymore. For fear of its inevitable loss." She stared hard at the window, and into the dark, wet world beyond it. "It sings despair in every cell of me."

She turned back to me and locked her eyes on mine.

"Do you know this feeling, Richard? Is it in you, too?"

"Yes," I answered. "I lost my wife and daughter. They were killed by a drunk driver. He killed himself in the crash as well. I had nothing."

"But you do now?"

"I have my work. I help people."

"You're not helping me."

"I'm trying."

"You're failing."

"If you want to stop meeting with me, just say the words. This only works if you want to keep trying. Do you?"

She let a deep breath bleed slowly from her lungs and was quiet for a while after. Between us, there was nothing but the layered small talk of a roomful of strangers, inane and without end; the white noise banter of a civilized society's slow but sure decline.

She pushed her hair from her face and looked directly at me and said, "Yes... I want to stop this hurting."

Chapter 10

Drip.

Droop.

Drip.

If I were to close my eyes I could believe it's raining, but it's not.

We are beneath the city and its inhabitants—underground, in a darkened sewer. Dripping from above us, and cascading down the walls on each side of us, are dark fluids of a questionable origin.

The smell of the place is both potent and foul, but my senses are numb enough for me to not be bothered by it. I'm far less concerned with the medley of rancid odors than I am interested in where we're going, and why we're going there.

The surface beneath us slopes downward slightly and we've been slowly descending for quite some time. Curving over us are walls of solid concrete, meeting at their uppermost point in a half cylinder. The base of the tunnel is flat but sunken slightly in the middle, allowing for a thin, shallow river of water and human waste to course quietly beside us.

Down the darkened tunnel Radey leads us with flashlight

in hand, wielding the circle of casted light like the lamp of a priest who is tending to some ancient burial chamber. The concrete above and below and on each side of us is becoming dark with mold, and the mold grows thicker and darker the deeper we go.

"You wish to find freedom from fear of death and pain," Radey says, and then is quiet.

I'm not sure if he's speaking in rhetoric, or asking a question to which he wants an answer. I wait a moment, then say, "As much as anybody, I guess."

He stops walking and turns to face me, saying, "Would you take your tender heart upon the heap of old age? To stand atop the skulls of all you destroyed to get there?"

I haven't the faintest clue how to respond to him.

We are both silent as he awaits his meaning to become clear to me. It doesn't.

He attempts to elaborate. "That which does not die cannot inflict death upon another. To find one's escape from the fevered realm of senses is to be cured of the illusory cycle of beginnings and ends; to let go of the self which is finite is to become joined with the self which is not."

"Do you really believe this stuff?"

His mouth curves to a smile. The sight of happiness upon his face is alarmingly off-putting. He turns from me and walks onward without an answer, and I follow in his steps.

The black puddle of a river is widening and soon I'm

having to lean against the concrete to keep to the furthest edge of the tunnel. I try my best to keep my feet dry. Still, my shoes are slipping into wetness.

As we make our way deeper, I find myself looking backward to the blindness; the lightless entirety of the way we've taken to get here. I think of how terrified I should be but am not. I imagine the bulb within the flashlight burning out. I imagine myself being enveloped in the blackness, with no means to escape it. Instead of feeling fear at such an idea, I become excited. I want to lose myself; I want to be nothing braced against nothing in the darkness.

I have a sudden, overwhelming urge to cause Radey psychological discomfort. "What about you? Can you die? You know you can die, right?" I feel like a child poking at a hornet's nest.

Radey stops walking. He turns slowly toward me, shining the light of the flashlight onto me as he does. While in the light I look to my hands. Both of them are black from touching the walls.

Radey doesn't answer, but from further down the tunnel there is a faint noise—an echo; the screech of an animal or the scraping of metal. It startles me, but Radey doesn't move or seem at all affected by it. He keeps the flashlight showing on me, while watching me intently. Then he lowers the flashlight slightly and as he does, I can see more clearly into his eyes. There is a vastness behind them; either an incalculable infinity of mental ruminations, or a total absence of any. Either way, it makes me incredibly nervous. My fearlessness of moments ago is beginning to crumble.

"Why did you bring me here?" I try to keep my voice from shaking, but do a poor job of it.

"To set you free."

If there's one thing I'm certain of, it's that I don't want to be set *free* by whatever means he's intending. "No, just stop. Tell me what we're doing here."

The faint screeching occurs again; this time louder, closer.

My nervousness is quickly becoming a full-blown panic attack.

"What the fuck is that sound?"

"The truth of what's to come is that you will only know the truth once you've no means to speak it."

"What the fuck is that supposed to mean?"

The shrieking occurs again, as if in response to my question. Once again, it is closer. My heart becomes a machine gun, shooting spurts of blood against my ribcage.

"Whatever you once were is not what you are, and that has always been the case, and it always will be... even on the day you die... and the day after."

The truth of the person before me becomes apparent, as obvious as it should have been prior to walking half a mile into a decrepit sewer system with him. "You are insane. Are you going to kill me?"

"Watch," he says.

He points the flashlight down the seemingly endless tunnel. At the fringe of the dull light's reach I catch a glimpse of a large moving shadow. It is there and then it's gone and I can no longer breathe.

"What was that?" My voice comes out a wheeze. It feels as though a noose is tightening around my throat.

"That," he says, "is your salvation." And then he shuts off the flashlight and there is nothing—no light, no form, no sound.

I can't help but think that if I die here then the suffocating blackness that surrounds us will become my mind eternal, and the thought is too terrifying to remain contained within me.

I try to speak out. I try to scream, but all that comes out is dead, soundless air. My legs are shaking wildly and it takes all my strength to keep them from buckling.

Radey's legs begin sifting through the water as he draws closer to me. I'm certain I'm moments from fainting. He stops moving when he's close enough I can feel the heat of his breath upon my face.

He whispers to me, and it's as if his voice is sounding from within my own skull.

"Souls are the eyes of God, and the body's death is but the blinking of an eye. Give yourself to death and you will become one with that which keeps on watching."

A terrible shriek sounds out from directly in front of me. At first I think it is the shrieking of a bird, but then I feel quite certain it is the sound of a woman screaming—the sound of a woman being murdered.

In response, something loosens inside me. I feel terrible fear and sadness. I feel I've done something terrible.

Electric adrenaline surges in my veins. Without a word I turn and run. My feet move of their own accord, carrying me through the pitch-black tunnel with frantic, panicked movements. I can only hope I'm headed back the way we'd come.

Lightless moments pass without any clarity of mind to document their passing, and I can't be sure that time even exists anymore. Fear and darkness have overwhelmed my every anchor to reality. More than once I trip and fall and writhe about in the foul fluids at my feet.

The minutes stretch into eons of hopeless panic and blind despair. I begin to think Radey may have already killed me. My thoughts are of the most pitiful and desperate sort. Please. Dear God, please. Let me get out of here. I will do anything. I will believe in anything if I get out of here.

A distant crack of light appears in the long darkness ahead of me. Salvation—pouring downward from a small circular opening which seems to lead to daylight. My eyes adjust and give form to a vaguely familiar ladder descending from the whiteness. I feel feral as I scramble toward it.

I grip the ladder's rusted handrails and ascend the rungs as fast as any Olympian would. I emerge from darkness into daylight and fall to the pavement beside the open manhole, huffing and puffing in dry rasping breaths. My heart is pounding so fast it would be impossible to count its beats.

I suck a deep breath of air into my lungs and then let it leak out of me slowly. I begin to feel as if I've just woken from a nightmare and all is well and I've nothing to be afraid of anymore. My heart begins to mellow in its beating; relief begins coursing through my veins, like a drug or sedative.

I'm in an alleyway and buildings stretch tall on every side of me. The world suddenly is tame and quiet, unthreatening, and I've never loved the sight of brick and mortar so much. It must be noon for the sun is high and bright and warm and blessed; this moment is a pleasantness beyond what any sentient creature deserves. There are birds singing somewhere above me, and cars droning in the distance.

I stand up and try to drag the manhole cover back into its place, but it's far too heavy. It seems impossible that Radey could have moved it. I stand above the darkened hole and listen for any sound from below. There is nothing but darkness and silence and I decide that's for the best. I leave the dark hole open and I head for home, not sure of what is real and what is not.

Chapter 11

Night has fallen with the light of the moon and stars hidden by cloud. Radey is standing within a darkened bedroom within a darkened house that is not his own. There is not a sound but that of his breath and beating heart and the occasional creaking of wood. A child sleeps soundly in a bed in front of him. It is a small boy; his body is hardly visible, lit only by the dull glow of an outside yard light.

The room is full with toys and entertainment. A computer. A TV. Books. The child's parents take care to keep their child obliged and happy. Radey watches the boy's miniature, softly breathing body with a blankness behind his eyes, all the while listening for any sounds denoting others awake within the house. There are none.

"The universe is a joke it played on itself," he whispers, and his voice flows through the quieted house much like wind flows through the leafless branches of dead trees. He takes silent steps toward the sleeping boy. "God was lost in the emptiness, and so he made the universe."

He walks until his legs are touching softly against the bed's edge. He looks down at the boy. "Do you hear me, little lamb? You are nothing but a witness poised to suffer the infinite voided dream of an entity who could no more care for you than I could for a cell which dies inside me. Do you hear me in your dreaming? You are a forgettable grain of sand in the dream of another."

He leans closer to the boy, close enough that his breath moves the child's hair as he whispers, "If you are allowed a future in this world, you will weep; you will weep for the stillness in your heart, and how it's been corrupted." He places his hand gently upon the boy's head, and proceeds to caress the boy's hair. The child turns in his blankets, making soft staccato groaning noises.

"The whole world is a cage; its bars are made from pain and fear, the likes of which have yet to lay their binds upon you. But rest assured, all that you love will be turned into nothing, and you'll be left to bear the pain of having lost it. Your body is but a tomb for all your coming sorrows. I am here to set you free from such a claim laid of you by God."

From his pocket Radey retrieves a lighter. He extends his arm so that his hand hovers above the boy's blanketed body. He flicks the lighter into flame. Soft, orange light fills the room.

Radey stares into the newly-opened eyes of the child before him. The child sits up in one instinctive, automatic motion.

He looks to be trying to scream but is too terrified to push sound from his fear-stricken lungs.

At the sight of the boy frozen in his trauma, a softness crosses over Radey's face, like a wave passing from the top of his head down to his jaw; emotion begins to show from him—sadness, and concern. He asks a question of himself aloud, in a voice soft and empathetic in tone.

"Who truly is the puppet in this moment? And for whose pleasure is this moment unfolding?"

His mind seems frozen as he contemplates the thought.

When he speaks again there is anger seething in his voice.

"I could kill you. I could kill you and your whole family."

His and the child's stares are both unblinking; each focused on the other. The house around them is quiet as a coffin.

A softer voice returns to Radey's lips, slipping calmly from his mouth. "Scream," it says. "Scream as loudly as you can and I will leave. I am just a bad dream."

The child heeds Radey's advice, letting out a terrible shriek.

Radey turns from the child and runs frantically, leaping through the opened window into the open world beyond it. He quickly becomes an apparition vanished into darkness.

Chapter 12

I wake to the sight of blue—a sky untouched by cloud, kissed by the morning sun. From every side of me there are threads of gold outstretched upward, waving back and forth in a gentle rhythmic motion.

I am flat upon my back with the cold feel of earth beneath me. The gold tendrils stretching upward are strands of tall field grass; they dance and sway in the pulse of a cool breeze. There is a dog barking somewhere in the distance.

Upon the skin of my right hand I feel a slight tickling sensation—that of a feather or a soft kiss. I lift my head to see a large black spider has taken to nesting upon my knuckles. Tiny eyes like jet-black beads are staring intently toward me. The small, fuzzy creature begins winding its two frontmost legs in the air in a circular motion, as if they're magic wands meant to cast a spell on me.

I lift my hand and move the creature closer to me. I rotate my hand slowly and it moves so as to stay atop and soon it is in my palm. I hold it close to my face and whisper, "You wouldn't hurt me, would you, fella?" It tenses its body against the feel of my breath. I have the odd desire to kiss it but decide it probably would in fact hurt me if I did.

I set it down to scamper in the undergrowth and then I stand up to scan my surroundings. Hilly golden fields surround me, and upon the horizon are the shadowed greens of pine tree forests. Down an incline not far from where I stand there is a wood and wire fence which runs along a pale brown dirt road.

I have no idea where I am or how I got here. The last thing I remember is making it home after taking a tumble in a sewage drain. I showered and changed my clothes and... oh, yeah... my father came home and I decided I'd rather sneak out than have him take notice of me.

My memory is blank of the moments that occurred after leaving the house, but it's apparent from my present situation I'd rather sleep alone in the dirt than spend another night in the same house as my father.

I walk to the small road ahead. I decide to follow it west, for no other reason than to keep the morning sun's blinding light behind me and out of my eyes.

There is a brisk breeze blowing in from the fields around me. My shadow stretches long down the road ahead, as if it is leading me onward. I think of Radey.

Is it possible to be aware of the fact that you are losing

your mind? Or isn't it some sort of requirement that it happens unbeknownst to you?

I decide to keep my mind grounded in the moment. I count my breaths. I allow myself to fully appreciate the sights and sounds of nature. Everything is shining in the morning sun's golden light; the world is growing more warm and gentle with every step I take. Everything is tranquil—everything but the damned dog I hear barking.

I leave the road and climb over the roadside fence and ascend a small hill thick with dry grass. Once atop the grassy embankment I see a house in the distance. Although it must be where the dog is barking, the area is suddenly, eerily quiet; there is not a single sound but the breathing wind.

The house is large and its walls are painted an unusually dark color—a shadowy gray, which would match perfectly the color of paper burned to ash. The framing for the house—that of the roof and windows and front door—is painted opaquely black, the color of coal. It is a strange sight and it's not hard to imagine it being the residence of someone crazed, and as such, I probably shouldn't continue approaching it, but—out of inexplicable curiosity—I do.

To reach the house I have to cross a small field of tilled but unseeded soil. Lying in the grass along the plot of loosened dirt are bags of seeds and farm tools, strewn about preparedly, awaiting humans hands to put them to their fated uses; but for some reason they sit neglected.

Perhaps the house has been overtaken by a sect of cultish people. Maybe they're cannibals, and they have no reason to reap the fields and yield such earthen bounties, as they've a basement full of human corpses ripe for consumption—the corpses of the house's former owners.

The idea of finding such a horror excites me deeply. I feel like a child, exploring an unknown world—a world of mystery, and danger.

As I draw closer to the homestead, a small boy exits the house through its front door. The child is young and small, perhaps five or six years old. His hair is the color of beach sand. He takes one look at me, then goes back inside the house. I take a moment to pause and consider what it is I'm really doing here; before I'm able to give myself a good answer, an older man comes out of the house. He marches toward me without any apprehension, like a soldier, or a madman intent on hurting me. Either way, it's probably best I get moving in the opposite direction.

I turn and start running, but something doesn't feel right.

My body feels weightless—ephemeral—as if I'm flying in a dream. When I look toward my feet I'm surprised to find I don't have any.

I panic. I move my hands to touch my torso, but find I have no torso to touch and no hands to touch with.

At first I am confused but then I begin to think I know what's happened.

I turn around and half-expect to see my body on the ground, dead. But instead I see myself standing before the man from the house. The man is holding a rifle to his shoulder and is pointing it at me—that is, he's pointing it at my body, which is standing right in front of me. The man appears sleepless and disheveled, with anger flaring from his eyes. His hair is an uncombed mess. He is dressed in pajamas and shouting obscenities.

What transpires is like a movie scene. I watch it from a distance; it plays out without my participation.

She who is Cathedra walks toward the man, slowly and without fear. The man shouts loudly at her, barking as fearsomely as he can muster, but Cathedra does not cower; she is not fazed in the slightest.

Once the man is within her reach she steals his weapon from him in one swift and terrible motion, yanking the gun from him as if tearing a feeble branch from a dead tree. The man squeals like a pig and quickly begins to plead for his life and the life of his child.

"Please, please, don't kill me. Don't kill us. I just want to protect my family." He waves his hands, as if they could stop a bullet. He takes a step backward and his foot catches upon a large jutting stone. He falls to the ground, landing on his backside. He whimpers like a wounded dog.

Cathedra asks the man a question, while pointing the gun at his crumpled body. "Are you a man of God?"

"Yes..." he says meekly.

She moves closer to him. "Then why are you so afraid to meet him? And your family? What have you to fear but God's grace bestowed to them if they're to die?" Cathedra points the gun directly at the man's head, then she lets it fall from her hands. It lands in the dirt by the man's feet. However, he does not attempt to pick it up.

Cathedra then says, "I came to apologize. I came back to assure you that I mean you no harm and you are safe. You can kill me if you believe it will make you feel safer, but I assure you it will not."

The man tries to speak but cannot; his vocal cords flap about uselessly, creating only gasping sounds.

"You've a lot in common with your son," Cathedra says. "You have his social skills." She turns from him and walks to the road. There is the faint rumble of a car upon it. Cathedra opens her mouth and speaks, saying, "Come now, Cathedra."

I heed her words, moving fast toward her until I am so close that I *become* her. Suddenly I am inside my body again. I look to my legs. I look to my arms and chest. Everything seems to be in its rightful place.

I am standing atop the grassy hill which overlooks the

road. Without a thought I start running toward the car which is fast approaching. I stumble frantically down the hillside, waving the vehicle down as I do. Once I reach the road it stops beside me.

A young man with a face made of pimples rolls down the window and asks if I need a ride. I turn and glance at the hill behind me. I wonder if a madman with a rifle will make his way over it before I can escape. I try to speak calmly when I say, "Yes. I do. That'd be great. Thanks."

I get into the car. The man starts driving before inquiring any further into my situation, and for that I am grateful. I keep watch out the window for the man with the gun but he doesn't come. I relax.

I ask the man where we are and he says the middle of nowhere. He asks what I'm doing here and I say I don't know. He asks if I'd like to be brought to town and I say yes.

We whir onward, down the dirt road. The sounds of rocks and gravel tossed about loudly by the car's tires accompany the hum of the engine.

"I think I know you from somewhere," the man shouts over the noise. "What's your name?"

"Cathedra."

"I'm Brad."

His friendliness makes me feel uneasy and I find myself looking to the backseat of his car for signs he's not a maniac or murderer. The floor is buried under fast food packaging and disposable used cups from coffee shops. Upon the seat are dozens of well worn books, all with mythical creatures or wizards or warriors elaborately drawn upon their covers. Brad is a nerd and this puts my mind at ease.

"Oh yeah!" Brad shouts over the rumble of the road beneath us. He waits for me to look in his direction. "The bookstore. I work at the mall. I saw you there. You were wearing the same black suit. Remember?"

"No."

"What's the deal with the suit anyway? You're not in some weird cult, are you?"

I'm starting to really hate Brad.

"Shut up about my clothes. It's none of your business." I stare out my window. I watch a small flock of wild birds soaring in the sky above a house in a field. There is an anger building inside me.

"Uh... I'm sorry. I didn't mean anything by it. It's just... interesting," he says.

"Where do you live?" I turn and stare hard into his eyes. "What is your address?"

"Huh? Why?"

He's beginning to squirm uncomfortably. I fight the urge to press him further. I fight the urge to go to his home in the night and burn it to the ground. "Nothing," I say. "Nevermind."

He drives me back to town, quiet the whole way. I have him drop me off near my house.

Chapter 13

Months earlier; an entry from Richard's private journal, stolen from his computer.

The sun was high and the sky blue but we were shaded from it. We walked a narrow beaten path in a densely wooded forest. Alongside us a river ran but was veiled from sight by foliage. There were thick tangles of branches, flowers, and berry brambles obscuring our view of pretty much everything but ourselves and the path we walked upon. It was quite beautiful and I was quite unused to such a setting.

Cathedra, however, was unusually comfortable in the context of nature, leading the way through the forest as an excited child would. "I can feel my fear is being lifted," she said as she bounced ahead of me.

"I thought being outside and in the woods might be... helpful."

"No. Not just right now," she corrected me. "I just mean in my life, altogether. I am becoming free."

"Oh? And why is that? What has changed?" My voice was beginning to show signs of concern for her state of mind.

"I found a way to move on. I found a way to stop hurting." She had to shout, so as to be heard over the sound of the river's rapids to our right. The torrent of rushing water had been growing louder as we'd been progressing further down the trail.

"This is good, right? This is what we've been working on." I shouted loud enough for her to hear me. We couldn't see it, as it was hidden entirely from view by the dense greenery, but we were near a waterfall. Its misty droplets had begun to saturate the air.

Cathedra stopped and looked back at me and waited for me to catch up to her. Then she moved close to me and planted her hands upon my shoulders. She leaned in and spoke into my ear. "You just have to accept the way things are and that you can never change anything. That is true freedom." Then she pulled away and I saw she was smiling brightly.

I began to feel certain she was experiencing a fit of mania, and I began to dread the fall in her mood that might be on its way.

"That sounds less like moving on and more like remaining still. That sounds like acquiescence. Are you sure you're feeling okay?"

She turned her back to me and rushed onward, shouting back her answer as she jogged ahead. "There is a distinct line between acceptance and acquiescence, Richard."

I followed her, and soon the woods opened up and we were ushered by the path to a rocky outcropping at the river's edge.

The walking path led alongside the rocks to a tall stone wall from which a waterfall spilled into the dark pool of water at its base. We walked upon the rocks and looked down at the white mist and swirling water below.

"I don't know," Cathedra shouted. "The way things are—right now—is natural. And we are designed to be impressed upon by nature. And who are we to argue with the flow of nature?"

She was dressed in a small blue dress that flapped in the breeze as she stood near the shallow rock cliff's edge.

"Sometimes the flow of nature leads us into suffering. Suffering that might've been avoided." I spoke my words quietly, as if embarrassed by them, and my voice went unheard, drowned out by the roaring of the waterfall.

"I can feel it inside me," she said, and she began to push the straps of her dress off her shoulders. "Flowing like a river." And her dress dropped to the rocks. "Beckoning me into a new way of living—ushering me into a new self. It feels... amazing, Richard."

And then she leapt off the rocks and into the water below and my heart stopped its beating. It wasn't such a great height—perhaps only five feet from the rocks to the water—but I felt as if she was falling to her death and I'd missed my chance to stop her. She fell like a stone and disappeared into the darkly churning water.

Panic filled my mind and yet I did nothing. I stood and

stared and waited, breathlessly.

She rose back up to the surface of the water, with a beaming smile upon her face. Her surroundings—the world that held her, the waters and rocks—suddenly seemed so dark in contrast to her fragile white body. The sight of her bare skin, naked as it was pale, made me feel fear for her safety, fear of the fiercest sort.

Behind her stood the monolithic wall of stone, which in that moment seemed ominous in appearance. The rocks were black from wetness and shadow all the way up to where they met the blueness of the sky. For all I knew, what Cathedra was doing was dangerous. The water fell from a great height above her and I didn't know how forceful the current was beneath her.

"Cathedra." I shouted loud enough for her to hear. "Are you sure this is safe?"

She was treading water and smiling.

"I'm better than ever, Richard. I'm happy."

"But this is... dangerous, isn't it?"

"I hope so," she shouted back.

And I sought quickly to draw her attention to something more grounded and familiar, however ridiculous it may have sounded in the context of the situation. "I've been meaning to ask, how has your job been lately? You're still working, right?" My shouting was a whisper amidst the roaring falls.

Her expression hardened into a frown. "What job?"

"At the mortuary. You talked about wanting to quit."

"What the fuck are you talking about?"

On her face was a deeply troubled look. She swam toward the rocks where I stood, her fun having clearly come to an end.

I asked her again if she felt okay. I told her she didn't seem herself and we should get her home. She lifted herself quietly from the water and climbed her way to me. It was then that I noticed the many bruises on her body—blotches of deep purple and gray markings, all across her torso, her upper arms, her thighs; the places bruises go when someone wants them hidden. I felt my concern for her welling up; my self-control was slipping from me. I felt sick inside for her.

"Cathedra. How did that happen? Who did that to you? Did someone do that to you?" I growled at her like any angry father would.

She stood slouched on the rocky outcropping. She was shivering like a frightened animal.

"My dad..." she said. "But he didn't mean to. It was an accident."

"Cathedra, this isn't funny. Don't play games with me. This is serious. Who did that to you?"

"You know what? Fuck you, Richard. I'm not playing games," she barked back. "You fucking asshole." She picked up her dress and slid it back onto her body. "I am feeling good and you are just trying to ruin it. You are trying to make me hurt just so you have someone to fix. Why can't you just let me be? I don't need you to be my fucking savior." She stood panting, her face red from anger. "Fuck you. Fuck you and your stupid dead family. I don't need you anymore. I will find someone else."

She walked past me, back to the path we'd come in on.

"Cathedra. You know if I suspect any abuse is taking place with any of my patients I have to report it."

I knew my words would be a leash she could not escape from. She froze then turned to face me.

"I have to," I said.

"You can't. You won't," she said.

"And why on earth wouldn't I?"

"If you do, I will never speak to you again." Her voice had become cold in tone; controlled and calculated. "Don't report it. It's not worth it, believe me. The bruises are nothing; an accident, and I need you. I will keep meeting with you. Please, just don't report anything."

I stood staring at her. The small blue dress was soaked wet—a second skin, glued to every contour of her body.

She'd begun walking toward me, and my heart had begun to morph into a wild animal, trapped inside my chest and beating rapidly as if it were trying to escape.

She'd sensed my control had slipped from me, and to her it was an opportunity to interact with me as she never had before, on equal footing—neither of us a patient and neither of us a therapist. She was enlivened by my desperation, my vulnerability. I was terrified.

She came near and hugged me. And then I was the one shivering. She kissed me on the cheek and I felt myself to be on the verge of crying. I pushed her away and said, "This isn't right."

"We're all going to die," she said. "At any moment. And then nothing matters anymore. Who's to say what's right. Just kiss me."

I lacked the strength to argue, and so I kissed her, and that night we slept together out in the woods—under blanket of blackness and stars, with the silhouettes of trees dancing through the night—amidst the world's windy whisperings and the sounds of animals traipsing the dark unknown all around us, until the sun would come again to push them back into hiding—amidst the singing shadows, lying naked with our arms and legs entwined as if we were one creature.

My mind comes alive in poetry at the mere thought of it. Those moments were the most fearless and free-minded of any I've ever experienced upon this earth.

Chapter 14

And so Brad lets me loose at the side of the road near my house and leaves without a word to me and I without a word to him.

The hour is twilight and night is approaching. Ahead of me is the sinking sun eclipsed by the sight of my house. Arcing over it, and over me, are the final scraps of the dying day—luminous veins of orange and gold and red light, wrought like the arms of lovers across the sky to entwine darkly with a scattering of purple clouds directly overhead. I take a deep breath of the cold air. A familiar feeling of gloom uncoils within me and I walk toward my home.

When I get inside I'm surprised at what I see, and hear. My father is cooking.

I can't remember the last time my father cooked a meal. I'm not sure he ever has. Yet here he is, busy building a feast; the kitchen noisy with the sounds of pots and plates being clanked about, and bacon sizzling upon the stove. Equally absurd is that the house is clean and well lit, with soft orange light like the light from candles filling every room. The kitchen and dining area and living room are all so unusually bright and warm and welcoming. And the smells. Powdered flour in the air. And maple syrup. And the rich scent of meat, browning in its heated oils.

My mother is seated at the dining table to my right, staring blankly at the empty air in front of me. My love for her is welling up inside me and I'm so happy to see her, regardless of the state she's in. I go to her and hug her and kiss the top of her head and say I'm sorry for being gone.

My father hears me and turns to face me. "It's okay," he says. "We're just glad you're home safe and sound." His hair is combed neatly to the side to reveal the entirety of his face and he smiles warmly at me, showing a type of vulnerability I didn't think him capable of. He appears truly grateful to see me, and happy to have me home, and it may cause me to break into tears.

This is home. And it actually feels like home, and I can't remember the last time I actually felt loved. "Sit down," my father says. "Supper's almost ready and something tells me you could use a decent meal."

I sit down and watch him as he cooks. It's not long before my eyes begin to wander... toward the living room floor. The spots of blood from the night prior have been cleaned from the carpet and it's as if they never existed. And now my father is humming a jovial, tuneless song within the kitchen.

What has changed in him?

It is a question I decide I don't want answered. I don't want to doubt something that feels so good inside me. I let gratitude flood through my veins like a drug.

So this is what a family is. So this is what love is, I think to myself. I'd almost forgotten.

Soon my father brings an empty plate to me. And then he brings a large plate stacked high with pancakes and bacon and eggs. He sets it at the center of the table and says, "Dig in."

And I do. I eat like a starved prisoner who's just recently been released from captivity and allowed to gorge themselves to their heart's content. I eat like I've never eaten before, until my belly is bloated and I can eat no more.

Sitting plump as Buddha—with night veiling down upon the world outside—I look to my father. He is seated directly across from me and I'm not sure he has touched the food before us. I feel guilty for having eaten without paying any mind to him.

He is staring at me and I begin to feel ill at ease. His eyes are cold and empty—inescapable black holes. I don't want to imagine what goes on behind them. Radey comes to mind.

As I'm sitting wondering what his game is—what the catch to all this is—he begins nodding his head, up and down and up and down. Over and over again in repetition and I feel nauseous. His lips curve into a smile.

I ask to be excused from the table. I hurry down the hall

and slip into the familiar seclusion of my room. With the sound of the door clicking shut behind me and the lock's tumblers snapping into place, I breathe a breath of relief. I'm locked in and the world's locked out. I leave the lights off and get into bed, blanketed by the darkness.

Cast inward by the moon's light outside my window is the wavering shadow of an apple tree, slinking slowly back and forth, its web of shadowed branches stretching all throughout my room.

You can't see the wind, I think to myself, only its effect upon the object impressed upon. And by what intentless wind am I shifted? And my father? By what mysterious light has such a shadow been cast over us?

My eyelids slink shut and my body begins sinking toward the cusp of sleep, but a gentle rapping at my window wakes me. My blood flutters, like a trapped bird's panicked wings, because I know it's Radey and he's come to kill me.

Go away. Go away. You're not real. My thoughts are like a useless house of twigs; I'm but a little pig and he a wolf. Nothing I could ever do would keep him out or keep me safe.

The window slides open and he slips in silent as a shadow. He's but a few feet from the foot of my bed, standing as a featureless shape of darkness, and I'm not sure why but I don't move or make a sound. Perhaps I'm too scared or I'm too tired. Or perhaps I believe I'm dreaming. But I haven't got it in me to resist his presence.

He walks beside the bed and kneels at its side. I turn my head and try to look into his eyes but it is too dark to see the details of his face. Behind him is a half moon beaming bright and yellow through the window. I can hear his breathing, he's so close.

"So fragile," he says, with a voice soft and gentle. "I'm not here to harm you. I only wish to wake you from your dream."

I try to speak but I find my tongue's too tired to form the words, and what words would I speak anyway?

"The days each hurt so much, don't they? Each one more wicked than the last; your mind so confined to this cycle of repeated suffering. I'm only here to bear the burden. You can give yourself to me and it can all go away. You won't have to be afraid, ever again."

"No..." I muster a breathless whisper.

He sighs and stands up. "Perhaps if I can make you see what I have seen," he says. "You will understand there are things more deserving of your fear than I." He reaches out his hand and presses it to my forehead. I can feel the warmth of blood behind his palm.

I don't think I'm dreaming.

"Witness clearly the world within you—a world which is beyond your means of controlling it." He is standing over me and staring down at me and it's hard not to think of him as a snake or some malevolent demon.

"Relax," he says. "You are tired of fighting—tired of

defending. Just surrender and it will all be over."

I try hard to keep my eyes from closing, but my vision is blurring and my body wants nothing more than to fall asleep.

"There is nothing to be afraid of," he says softly. "Feel the warmth within my hand and just... let go."

And with his words, all my mind's churnings come to a halt.

Chapter 15

The world is veiled in a brilliant unmoving mist—a congealed smoke, enshrouding everything in whiteness. Almost everything—all but the brown blades of dead grass beneath my feet and the darker brown of earth beneath the grass and a large dark tree which stands a short distance ahead of me.

The sight of the shadowy tree rouses a familiar feeling within me, vague and nagging like déjà vu. I try to find the memory from whence the feeling flows but such is the source that it eludes me, much like whatever forms are hidden by the formless white all around.

The feeling grows; the feeling is dread. I am terrified, and the terror grows more with every moment I spend staring at the tree. So much so that it becomes unbearable and I want to turn and run but I am afraid that if I do I will be lost in the smoke forever.

I tell myself I'm dreaming and I've no reason to be afraid.

None of this is real and what is not real cannot hurt me.

I walk toward the tree and when I am close enough to touch it I see its bark is not bark at all but a thick red, flowing fluid—a flue of crimson liquid, alive and coursing, formed to shape the tree's trunk. Gently it convulses and churns, defying any notion of gravity.

Reaching out from the tree's trunk are snakes, dark and rigid and formed into the shapes of tangled branches. From the snakes, erupting from their darkly scaled skin, are leaves of fire. Thick in the air is the smell of cooked flesh, and I know suddenly that the tangled black snakes, stretching upward as far as I can see, are the source of the smoke that covers up this dreamscape. Each of them erupting into flames and being cooked alive; their torment obscuring all the world but that of their own suffering.

As I'm staring at the churning blood of the trunk of the tree and fighting the sudden inexplicable urge to reach out my hand and touch it to feel what's inside, I feel something brush against my shoulder and I jump back, aghast.

Hanging down from the largest of the serpentine branches is a small dark object at the end of a long rope. It swings back and forth as if there is a breeze but there is none. I look more closely at it and see the dark object is the lifeless body of a mangled raven. A small rope is wrapped around its neck. Its body is dripping drops of blood onto the ground.

And I know now the raven's blood is what feeds the tree.

I know it to be the ceaseless cycle—the ceaseless source—of all my suffering, and my heart caves under the inescapable truth of it. I lie beneath the tree and wish it to take my blood and for the dream to be over with.

Chapter 16

My eyes are open but the world is dark. My breath is slow
and my heart is hardly beating. I am cold. My body is tightly
curled, like an unborn fetus still enwombed in the lightless realm
of their mother's innards. I am reluctant to try and move for fear
that I won't be able to.

I stretch out my legs and roll onto my back. I wriggle my
arms about then clench and unclench my fingers. Every muscle
within me aches. I feel like I've been hit by a truck. My head
throbs and there is not a single identifiable emotion within me.

I realize I am upon a bed and under blankets. I slide out
from under the covers and stand up in the harsh light of my
bedroom. The early sun pouring through the window shows me
that I am naked.

The floor is cold beneath my feet as I walk from the bed to
my closet. Dangling from hangers within it are an assortment of
shirts and pants and dresses. I push them all aside and reach
deeper into the closet. Behind my normal clothes is a single black

suit, wrapped in plastic and hanging secretly.

I pull it down and dress myself in it then leave my room and walk down the hall toward the kitchen. I can hear my father cursing the world as he struggles to find something in a cupboard. Then there is a crashing of pots and pans onto the floor.

"God damn it. Who the fuck put these here?" He poses his question angrily to the lifeless air around him, and grows more angry when it doesn't answer.

I step into the kitchen and see him on his knees, collecting the fallen pots and pans.

"Having problems?" I ask and smile at him.

He looks up and stares at me like I've just done the single worst thing I could possibly do to make him more angry.

"Did you put these here?" His eyes are filled with fire—the unblinking predatorial stare of hatred.

"What does it matter if I did? Regardless of how they got there, you are still in this predicament. Deal with it." I clench my lips and try to hold back my laughter, but it slips out anyway.

He lunges to his feet and stands within arm's reach of me. He gives me his worst, most hideous, angry-gorilla stare.

"Do you think my discomfort is funny?" he growls.

"Yes," I say.

And then he throws his arm out to punch or slap me and I move out of the way. He loses his balance and his body stumbles forward. He trips over his own legs and smashes his face hard against the kitchen counter's edge, then he crumples to the floor. There is blood on the countertop. He lies motionless on the floor like a stunned deer who's just been hit by a car.

I kneel beside him and say into his ear, "It's one of the benefits of being severely depressed. I have no fear. So you have no power over me. My pity for you has all but dried up."

There is no response from him, only his soft, slow breathing.

I stand up and say, "You are pathetic and only have yourself to blame for everything wrong in your life," and then I leave him lying on the floor in a puddle of his blood and I walk to the living room.

My mother is in her wheelchair. She sits with the living room window behind her and her eyes facing the kitchen. She's but a monument to all I find sorrowful about the world—a hollowed statue of her former self, nothing within her but that which I project there.

I crouch beside her and say, "Mom, I've got nothing left—all my feelings, all my love—it's all been burned away inside me."

And then I sit staring into her oceanic marble eyes until I'm certain there's nothing behind them anymore. I stand and walk to the door and exit the house. As I'm walking down the street and away from the only home I can remember knowing, I feel with certainty that I will never see her, or my father, ever again.

And for the first time in my life, I'm okay with that.

Chapter 17

*Months earlier; an entry from Richard's private
journal, stolen from his computer.*

There was a man on the television in the room we were in.
A starship captain engaged in a one-on-one battle with some sort
of lizard-man on a barren desert-like planet. The two of them
were stranded and without weapons, forced to fight one another
with whatever they could scavenge from their environment. The
lizard-man had found a large piece of wood which he looked
intent on battering the man with.

The television's sound was off and Cathedra watched it
with a look upon her face I could not decipher; either boredom or
deep interest. Our bodies were side by side upon a spring
mattress bed, the both of us clothed only by a thin layer of
blanketing which was wet from the sweat of prior moments.

Outside our hotel room it was raining, and it had been for
hours. Inside, the room was lit dimly by a single orange bulb that
occasionally flickered on and off. The walls of the room smelled of
ash and smoke—no doubt from thousands of lit cigarettes having
passed through the lips of strangers in their midst. The ceiling

was blotched with brown stains from rain that had leaked in through the roof over the years. A white bucket sat at the center of the room catching drips of water as we watched the television program.

Cathedra laughed dryly at the sight of the man and the lizard-man and their unfolding drama. Then she turned to me and said, "When I was a kid, I thought I was a good person. Now I know I'm not. There's this... darkness growing in me. With every single fucking breath I take on this fucking planet it grows in strength. It's like the very universe is evil at its core—designed to mold all things in its image, and I'm no exception."

The badly-costumed, rubbery-faced lizard-man had gotten the starship captain into a vulnerable position. He'd lost his weapon—the scavenged piece of wood—but somehow he'd gotten the captain into his arms and was squeezing him tightly.

"Richard. I'm starting to get these impulses... I'm starting to want to hurt people, for no reason other than to watch them hurt."

And to think I'd thought she might have been enjoying herself. I stared blankly at the TV screen and my mind scrambled for words to offer some sort of consolation.

"It's perfectly fine to get angry," I said.

The starship captain fought free from the lizard-man's hold and escaped to a distance, where he found a large rock, which he hurled back at his adversary. However the stone simply bounced off the lizard-man's torso, as if he were invulnerable—as if he were made of mountain.

"These are normal human emotions, you know."

Cathedra erupted into laughter, dispelling any notion that she had any interest in my words; her eyes were locked in a dead stare toward the TV.

Still, I went on talking.

"Perhaps you just need to find a way to more regularly express your darker emotions—to get them out of you so you don't have to suffer through them alone. Perhaps you can find an outlet. Maybe writing, or painting; art can provide a release."

"No. I mean I *really* want to hurt people." Her voice grew more forceful. "This goes beyond feeling mad and writing in my fucking journal about it." She drew a slow deep breath and closed her eyes, as if to focus her thoughts.

And then her words came out in a calm whisper, spoken without emotion, spoken as if she'd suddenly become possessed by the voice of another.

"I want to destroy everything you people hold dear. I want to watch the pain behind your eyes as you lose everything. You mean nothing to me. I want to watch you burn as you lose everything you thought yourself entitled to."

Silence engulfed the air between us. On the television the lizard-man had picked up an enormous boulder which he hurled toward the man. The man dodged it, made an escape—and then

Cathedra said, in a voice that was more her own, "Is that normal? I really don't think that's normal, Richard."

"What do you mean when you say, *you people*?" I pondered for a moment how to phrase the next question without further rousing her hostility. "Cathedra, how would you feel if *you* lost everything?"

"I've already lost everything."

"Do you want *me* to lose everything?"

The room's lighting flickered off then on, the power having shorted out for only a split second. When it came back on the TV had lost its channel; white noise static shone on its screen and hissed quietly from its speakers. Outside the hotel there were the dull rumblings of thunder somewhere distant but approaching.

"So you want everyone in the world to feel the same sense of loss that you do? Is that it?" I asked.

She didn't answer. Instead she began recounting a memory while staring blankly out the room's single large window. The glassed view was wet with rain, offering nothing but a blur of grayness for her to gaze into.

"The other day in town I saw a broken-down old homeless man begging from a dirty streetside corner." She spoke as if recalling some distant trauma that was difficult to revisit. "I watched this poor, broken person as he asked another man kindly for some change. The man he asked was dressed nicely and most certainly had money to spare, but still the richer man ignored the needs of the older, destitute man. He looked him in the eyes—was empathetic with him, he even apologized—but he didn't give him anything. No money. Nothing."

Her voice trembled as she spoke.

"This feeling swept over me. I just became... enraged. I fantasized just... awful things. I imagined myself just tearing this guy to pieces with my bare hands—clawing into his skin and pulling his insides apart—just turning him into a bloody pulp of body parts and bone. I wanted to turn him into nothing, but not before I'd tortured him so severely that such a death would be a gift. And that's not even the worst of it... The worst part is that thinking about it right now is making me excited."

"What do you mean, excited?"

"Like—sexually. It turns me on."

After hearing her words I found myself struggling to suppress my own feelings of arousal.

A rapid succession of lightning flashes soundlessly filled the room as I spoke my next words. "Cathedra. It's not always what we feel that is important, but what we do with those feelings." And after the strobing whiteness was gone, the room was without electricity; the bulb above us dead of its soft buzz and orange glow.

"What if it's not our choice what we do." Her voice was a meek whisper in the darkness.

"What do you mean?"

She let out a toneless laugh and said, "There's a lapse in my memory that day where I can't remember what happened. I just totally... blacked out. I remember following the man as he walked along a street and into a store—a jewelry store. I felt my anger growing for him—this man who had no money for a beggar who was starved and suffering, but could apparently spare his precious dollars for some useless decorative object."

Cathedra stopped talking and instead just lay still on the bed beside me. She groaned as if in pain, while still staring away from me, toward the gray and rainy world outside.

Minutes passed with her not talking before I broke the silence. "Cathedra?"

"For all I know...." She breathed heavily, as if catching her breath, and I could tell by the sound of her voice she'd begun to cry. "He could've been buying a wedding ring for someone he loved. Maybe he was a decent caring person, but at the time I felt nothing but rage for him; I didn't care. I followed him into the store and that's when I blacked out."

"And then what happened?"

"How the fuck should I know?" She belted out her words angrily. "I said I blacked out. For all I know I killed him. The next thing I remember is I was running and panting in an alleyway. I had his wallet and it was loaded with cash. I was so scared I threw it in a dumpster and just ran home. Ever since it happened, I've been watching the news... checking online... just waiting to hear something bad... but there's been nothing. It's like it didn't even happen. But I know *something* happened. I had his wallet."

She turned to look at me in the darkness. Her face was shadowed enough that I couldn't see its expression, but I could see her cheeks were wet with tears. "I'm scared," she whispered. "I'm scared I did something bad. It feels like something terrible happened but I don't know what."

"This man..." I knew my next words would be a risk. "Did he remind you of your father?"

She jerked up and sat rigidly upon the bed, the white bed sheets slipping off her as she did. Darker than the dark gray sky of the windowed world behind her was the silhouette of her naked body in front of me. I traced its outline with my eyes and once again struggled to stomach my own feelings of sexual arousal.

"What the fuck does that have to do with anything?" she growled.

A series of flashes lit the room and for a moment it was as if the electricity was back on. Cathedra's pale naked skin was lit up bright as day and for a few fleeting moments I savored the sight, and then the both of us were left blind in aftermath of the white light's passing.

"Cathedra, listen. I'm on your side. We're in the thick of this together now. And I am not the enemy. You can trust me. I only want to help you."

I spoke my words into the formless dark and just as I

finished speaking them a violent thunder tore through the skies outside our little room. The hotel shook. It was the sound of mountains exploding. Cathedra reacted to it about as much as a statue would, completely unsurprised and unfazed by such jarring, horrific sounds. I reached out and set my hand gently on her back to try and comfort her. My touch made her wince, more startling than the sound of the air itself exploding moments ago.

"I trust you," I said, trying to be reassuring. "I trust you to do good, to the best of your abilities. And from the sound of it, you didn't hurt anyone. You took money from a man who was apathetic to the needs of another man. And even then you felt guilt for what you'd done."

I sat up next to her. I put my arm around her. I pressed my naked skin against hers.

"This is what we're gonna do," I whispered, and kissed her on the cheek. "We're going to continue to explore this anger—this desire to hurt other people. We're going to really put a face on it, and get to know it and where it came from." I kissed her again. "And in doing so I promise it will become more... manageable; it won't be something to be afraid of. It will just take some time. Okay?"

She closed her eyes and I felt her muscles relax, go limp. Her body leaned into mine. She let out a deep breath and a fresh tear rolled down her cheek where I'd just kissed her. I pressed my tongue onto the bare skin of her shoulder. I tasted her neck. I licked the skin of it, tracing my tongue all the way to the wetness of the tear upon her cheek. I lapped up the salty remnants of her sorrow, no longer able or willing to hold back the urge to fuck her.

"Okay," she said.

Chapter 18

I am not afraid. Of anything. I have nothing to lose and nothing to gain. My mind all the more clear because of it. My wallet, my money, my identity—all left at the house that once was mine but is no longer.

Free of any obligation to a home or an identity, I am no longer anchored in reality, and I plan to drift unhindered until the world reveals a purpose for me, and that purpose will be all the identity I need. My every action will unfurl at each new moment's beckoning, without a second guess from fear or hesitation. I came from nothing and to it I will return. Of what use is fear and apprehension in between? My every breath a blessing I've no right to claim or grow attached to.

All around me, the city is waking—its ant-like humans returning to their bustle of work and school and delusions, all of which never seem to lead to any meaning or end, save for death. The system that imprisons them all is but a game. The reward is nothing but a prompt ending of their lives.

I will not participate. I will not fall victim. Walking the streets in the early morning light, I am without intent to serve within this mechanism of society. I am free, because I know I have a greater calling.

Duplicate houses and stores and business buildings are all lined up in rows along the busy streets; I pass the prisons, watching the people within them as if they are animals trapped in a zoo of their own making—every human inhabitant of this design seemingly unknowing of the freedom being denied them.

A new purpose is beginning to take form within me. I am here to wake them—to set them free from their complacency. Like any animal, they just need a little... push. A little flame alight beneath their creature comforts to jar them into living freely.

It's still early when I reach the outskirts of the city's center. The sun is but a low-hanging orange ember still veiled by the horizon, the pale morning light diffused by buildings of brick and stone outstretched as monolithic silhouettes ahead of me.

I know I'm searching for something specific. But I also know I won't know what that something is until I see it. I make my way to a busy street corner and set myself upon a bench in front of a store. Behind me teenagers talk about work and school and things they hate, namely work and school. In front of me two men of an older generation are standing talking about how times have changed and people are so different now. I'm thinking how it's all the same—still everybody self-obsessed and trampled on by fear and comfort. Nobody living free. Except for me.

And then I see it—this moment's purpose. Across the street I sight a woman radiating strength and determination amidst a crowd of slow-moving, depressed-looking people. The woman is dressed all in black, presumably business attire. Her feet slap like horse hooves against the concrete sidewalk as she marches through the other humans, regarding each of them as if they are her subordinates.

I stand and cross the street and follow her.

She enters into a bright-lit store. Flashing lights and colorful banners beam outward from its windows. The usual advertisements for anatomically-mutated superheroes and Barbie doll figures thin enough to be near death but still glowing with the most confident of smiles. A toy store. The future basis for our children's delusions and depression. The place where children choose their idols.

Door chimes sing to me as I open the store's glass entry door. A cloud of perfume wafts over me. To my right I catch a glimpse of the business woman's darkly clothed body. She's a shadow, quickly slipping down an aisle and out of sight.

I follow the trail of her perfume and turn down the same aisle. And there she is, eyeing the rows of packaged action figures and tapping her foot impatiently. She doesn't take any notice of me. I may as well be a ghost.

Dangling at her backside is a small black purse from which

she pulls a cell phone. She opens the phone in her palm and lets go of the purse so that it rocks back and forth like a pendulum.

I slip behind her. And suddenly I'm close enough to breathe her scent—to feel her body's heat. If she had the slightest awareness of the world around her she'd notice my hand is fingering through her personal belongings.

She puts the phone to her ear just as I slip a billfold from her purse.

"I'm here and I don't see what you asked for." She is clearly angry with whomever she has called. She expels forced and labored breaths so as to express her discontent. "They don't have it. Tell me something they have and you want or I'm leaving and you're getting nothing."

She is quiet as she listens. I can't make out what the person on the other end is saying in response but it sounds like a child's voice.

"Ugh... fucking pathetic." She presses the cell phone shut and drops it into her purse then turns to face me.

"What the fuck are you looking at, freak?"

I smile and say, "A coward."

"Excuse me?"

Her eyes are locked upon my face, as if contained behind it is the cause of every pain she's ever suffered. I could have blood dripping from my hands and she wouldn't notice. Which is good, because I am still holding her billfold. I put it calmly into my pocket and continue talking without her noticing that what was hers is now mine.

"To what end do you treat yourself and others with such disdain?" I ask. "The world is not yours to own. Every moment is a gift deserving of your embrace and gratitude, yet you shy away from it." I must look and sound like some Christian missionary prepared to give a sermon, dressed in my black suit.

Her anger gives way to confusion. She is flustered and doesn't know what she's dealing with. She rolls her eyes and shakes her head then simply walks away, mumbling to herself.

A chimed melody rings through the store as she pushes her way through the glass door to the outside world. I hear her talking to herself, and to anyone unfortunate enough to be within her vicinity. "Fucking psycho. I swear everyone in this city is a lunatic but me." And then there is the sound of sucking air as the door shuts behind her.

I stand alone in the aisle and look through the contents of her billfold. Nearly a thousand dollars in cash. Half a dozen credit cards. And most importantly, her driver's license.

Her address.

I'll wait a few days, maybe a week. Until she's gotten over the trauma of having been robbed. Then I'll go to her house and burn it to the ground.

Chapter 19

The moon hangs hidden somewhere behind the towering architecture that looms on every side of me. The sun has sunk, and beyond the hazy darkness that overshadows the city's lights the stars still shine but I can't see them.

I sit waiting like a lion on the prowl, in a lightless alley where the air smells like grease and garbage. The sounds are those of cars cutting through the nighttime air and the occasional voices of passersby on the nearby street and also the whispers of the suffering homeless in the darkness even closer.

It's hard to tell how many broken humans lurk in this darkened crack with me—between the buildings where the hived humans spend their fleeting daytime hours doing trivial tasks for sake of dreamed-up glory—but there are more than a few. In the moments when the noises of the city become quieted I can hear their dry whisperings, or sometimes they cough or rustle softly in their beds of garbage.

I can't say with certainty which is worse off. These bodies

lying beaten in the darkness, starved of sustenance and love; or the fattened humans working off a debt to a dream that exists only in an imagined future. Both lie sleeping and both are awaiting someone to wake them to the truth. The truth being that they are free and need not suffer to their deaths like trapped rats in some unending failed experiment.

"Dude! I want to find someone to fucking fight." It is a young man's voice. One of many from a crowd that is out of sight, somewhere beyond the alley's entrance, walking along the street nearest me. There is laughing and shouting and the usual sounds of drunken masculinity. And the sounds are growing closer. I sit crouched and listening, veiled in shadow beside a dumpster.

"Yeah. Let's fuckin do it. The next person we see, let's just beat the shit out of them." A chorus of laughter echoes loudly through the alley. They are almost upon the alleyway's entrance.

I stand and walk toward the sound of their shouting, toward the light of streetlamps and flickering neon business signs.

"Don't go out there." A voice like gravel pleads from a shadow near my feet. I can hardly make out the man's body beneath a pile of tattered rags and clothes. "Please." Each of his words is a coughed-out whisper. "They mean it. They will hurt you. Just get down and hide and they'll move on."

I walk past the man and step onto the brightly lit sidewalk. I turn and face the group of stylishly dressed young men. They continue talking and laughing, taking a few more stumbling steps before they take notice of me.

Their voices become quiet as they stop to look at me.

There are perhaps ten of them. All dressed in check-marked canvas sneakers and tight-fitting jeans and sweaters. They whisper quietly to one another and then exchange nods. I simply stand there breathing. Huffing, really. I most certainly look like a maniac—crawled from the depths of some dark alleyway, in a black suit that is now stained and stinking.

"Yo bitch," the leader of the group barks, "you lookin for some fun?" His eyes are lit with the confidence of a short life lived always in the spotlight of his friends and secluded social circle. "You wanna get fucked up? Or maybe you just wanna get fucked." His friends laugh.

Inside me there is a faint whisper of fear rising up, but I bite down on my tongue to keep it quiet. The pain makes me feel stronger, more in control.

"I'm looking for a lost child," I say. And some of the group pause from laughing to exchange confused looks. I continue talking and begin walking slowly toward them. "This child... he forgot his nature. He forgot he's forgotten." I speak my words coolly. I look upward at the muted night sky and then back at the group and continue as if in a casual conversation with friends. "This child once was awake and now he sleeps his life away. Given in, he has, to the delusion that he is somehow protected from the doom that impends on all of us. I think this child is you."

"Yo bitch, are you off your meds or something?" The alpha male speaks his words and then looks to his friends for their approval. Some of them are laughing, some are looking more confused now as to the nature of our exchange.

"I have seen death and no medication or amount of ignorance can take its vision from me," I say, loud enough that it shuts them all up. "What greater thing than death do you possess that you hope to threaten me with?"

As I speak these words there is a fear rising up in me again, not in response to the men in front of me but in response to the words themselves. I realize that I have, in fact, seen death. I bite into my tongue again, harder this time. I taste blood. And then I speak my words in a voice steeled of such confidence it doesn't allow the option of not being listened to.

"My heart is a thing of the timeless and you are but a child abandoned and unloved, afraid of a world you do not know." I am close enough they can surely see the sorry state of my attire and perhaps can smell me too. There is a look of concern growing across all their faces. I can feel for the first time I have total power over the situation. They are afraid of me.

"You seek to perpetuate a reality where all that you are fearful of remains hidden from you," I say. I speak my words so forcefully that spit sprays from my mouth. I can feel it running down my chin. "You want a world where you bear witness only to that which is familiar and comforting." I am close enough that I could reach out and touch the leader. I could attack him. I could kill him.

Some of the group are beginning to back off. I growl my next words. "You are a coward hiding amidst a culture of denial, and I am here to take you from a life not worth living."

One of the alpha male's posse reaches his hand out and places it upon the leader's chest, pushing him back slightly, saying, "Yo dude, let's not even fuck with this shit."

"Yeah," he agrees. "This is just... fuck this."

They begin shuffling backward while keeping their eyes on me. I stand my ground and when they've reached a good distance from me they turn their backs to me and continue walking away.

My heart is thumping against my ribcage and when I look down I see my shirt is absolutely soaked with fresh blood. For a moment I think I've been shot or stabbed and that somehow it happened unbeknownst to me. Then I realize it is coming from my mouth. I've bitten into my tongue too deeply and blood is gushing from the wound, draining down my chin, and it must have been doing so for quite some time now. A wicked smile sets across my face.

I go back to the alley from whence I came and curl up in the shadows, contented.

The world is mine and I am not afraid of anything. I am free to follow my heart's each and every bidding without regard for consequence; death has no bearing on me anymore, and for it I've no fear. These are my final thoughts before consciousness wanes and I fall into a dark and peaceful sleep.

Chapter 20

*Weeks earlier; an entry from Richard's private
journal, stolen from his computer.*

"You can't keep doing this, Cathedra. This needs to stop."

She'd showed up at my office early in the morning, clearly
falling apart emotionally. Seeking refuge not in a therapeutic
session but in our personal relationship. Her jeans were stained
with mud and her eyes were sunken and sleepless. She smelled of
smoke and the fresh air of nature, like she'd been camping.

"Richard... something is happening to me and I'm scared.
Those... impulses I'd told you about, they're getting worse." She
sat herself upon the couch as usual and I sat down in the chair
across from her. A world of empty space between us. The way my
job dictated it had to be.

"Did you black out again?" I asked.

She didn't answer. Instead she rose and walked over to me
and stood next to me. The smell of smoke was thick in the air
around her, and also a faint trace of gasoline. She reached for my
hand but I pulled it away and told her again this needed to stop.
Behind her eyes was a world of barely masked emotions nearly

brimming and spilling out of her—an anguished desperation, a fire seething.

"I told you before. This—this relationship existing outside the boundaries of therapy—needs to stop. It's getting out of control and it's not helping either of us."

She stared at me, her body quivering from what I could only assume was rage. A tear slid from her eye and ran down her face, dripped to the floor.

"Why do you smell like fire? Have you been camping?"

She acted as if I'd not even spoken and instead shifted the focus onto me. "Are you really such a coward?" Her voice was a timid, broken whisper. "All you have to do to help me is be here for me, as a real person—not some professional doing it for money. You like to think it's separate—that I'm a patient and you're a doctor and there's no emotional connection—but that's not how it works."

"Cathedra. It's not that simple. You've become emotionally entangled with me, in an unhealthy way. And I can't allow those feelings to grow. Okay? I'm here for you, but as your therapist. Nothing more. I need you to be calm and strong. I need you to sit down and talk through this with me."

"Please... don't do this to me, Richard. This was the only thing I had left. Please."

"This is not about our relationship. This is about you. You are in a very serious situation and we have to deal with it."

"God damn it, I don't have a *situation*. I just have pain. Like everybody else.... Like you. And you think pushing me away will help? You think treating me like some customer is really what I need?"

Her voice was raised and in response I raised mine. "Really? You don't have a situation? Care to talk about your parents, then?"

She closed her eyes, became rigid and held her breath. Then after a few moments of utter silence throughout the room, a squeak leaked from her mouth like a balloon with a hole poked into it. And then came tears. Streaming from her eyes. Her face flushed with red. Her body shaking.

"Yes. I know they're dead. Okay, Richard. I know they're dead. I know I was a child when it happened. I know it's not my fault and there's nothing I can do to change what happened. So fucking what if I want to believe they're not dead. Is that so bad? Is it so bad I want to believe the world's a better place than it is?"

"It's one thing to 'want' to believe something. It's another to lose sight of reality entirely." I watched her as she breathed heavily, her lungs heaving air as if it were poison. "You told me your father was beating you, Cathedra. Did you know your parents were dead when you said that? On several occasions you've talked about them as if they were still alive. Do you remember any of that? You do, in fact, have a 'situation,' Cathedra. The world you're choosing to believe in is not, in fact, a better one."

On her face was the look of a helpless child out of words to plead with.

"Listen. Come here." I stood up and moved close to her and took her in my arms. "It's going to be okay. I won't abandon you, ever. We will get through this together." She was shivering in my arms.

Then she tried to kiss me and I pushed her away.

She stood there staring at me. Coldness behind her eyes. The flow of tears gone abruptly. She flashed at me a look of disgust and then turned and left without a word, ignoring my pleas for her to stay.

Chapter 21

Chaos, unbridled and violent, is erupting behind me. There are shrieks and screams and the muffled patterings of feet across carpeted floor. It is a small squad of children running and shouting in the room behind me. Their mania continues until a hoarse-voiced woman scolds them and tells them to keep quiet.

The lighting here reminds me of every department store I've ever been in, but here the floors are carpeted softly and the room is broken into segmented rows of shelves filled not by products for purpose of profit, but instead by typewritten information for information's sake; books upon books, forgotten and dusty within their tended tomb. I am in a library.

Sitting here in this large and now quiet room I can feel my livelihood is in jeopardy; my steam is running thin. Once again the fault is Richard's.

In the past few days, I've robbed a woman. I've stood my ground against a group of malevolent frat boys. I've faced fear and found my purpose.

I am an agent of truth, put upon this earth to steal delusions from the sleepers—here to wake them from the lies that necessitate their slumber.

But now something has slowed my mission. The gears are grinding down, nearly to a halt. Here in this public library, sitting in front of a public computer, I'm reading about past moments I shared with Richard.

Within the pocket of my suit I found a small USB drive which I don't remember putting there, and stored within it are hundreds of recollected moments, typed by Richard, sometimes accompanied by recordings of his voice. Some of these moments I remember. Some I don't.

Of particular interest is an instance where I'd told Richard I knew my parents were dead. It is one of the final entries.

I don't know what to make of any of this.

But it's got me thinking I can let the sleepers sleep a day longer.

I owe my mother and father a visit.

Chapter 22

A fire flickers in my heart, like a candle dim. A lonely flame fading into darkness. My every trace of love soon to be nothing more than black ash scattered into blackness. There's just one last flicker left in me.

I enter into the house of my parents—the house I'd left just days ago—and find it empty. Beneath my feet is familiar carpet, gray and stained, once white but no longer. Dim rays of sun seep through the windows painting pale gray light over everything. Everything lifeless. All around me are the fake-wood paneled walls that look black from being unlit by artificial light.

It's midday and the only sounds are birds chirping softly in the outside air. Their muffled song voices tumble through the house and intrude on the otherwise silent air. The separateness of their singing serving to make the dead, walled-in space all the more lonely.

Of what use am I if I haven't an identity or a past to look back on? Who am I without regret?

Outside sits perched a lonely bird upon a branch of nature, blind of name and memory. Am I any better off? Of what song am I to be bloomed of ignorance, to toil in jovial snare until my death?

The house is more barren than I can ever remember. The furniture dusty. And a smell of must and faint rot hangs upon the air. The cupboards are all emptied of groceries and amenities. There's no sign that anybody's lived here in a long while.

And how does one cease to anger at a plot designed to lead us to defeat? And what else is all of life?

The living room and the kitchen and all rooms within the home lie unused… unused but as a home for my delusions.

I call out to the emptiness. "Mom! Dad!" And the words are useless lies I can no longer believe. They fall like dead flies in a window sill. There's nobody here but me. And I know it. I think I've always known it. I walk to the room I'd believed belonged to my parents. I open the door and look inside. It's as empty as the inside of me. No bed. No furniture. Nothing. Had I never bothered to look before? Would I have seen it as it is if I had?

Nausea unfurls inside me, like the wilted petals of a drowning flower coming undone. I trace the house as I remember it from just days earlier. Nothing is as it should be. Or perhaps everything is as it should be—my mind finally embracing the cold truth of reality.

In my room I find only a bed, nothing else. The closet is reft of any clothes; a single hanger dangling where my black suit must have hung. A faint sadness is welling up from somewhere deep inside me. I've nothing to return to, I can't help thinking. I'm stuck upon my path. The wheels are in their unstoppable motion. Inside me there is remorse faint but nevertheless calling out—its distant rapping like a raven at the edge of my consciousness.

"I got rid of your other clothes."

Radey's voice is hardly a surprise as it sounds out from behind me. I turn to see him sitting on the bed.

"And everything else. It's all gone now. You can't go back, you know. You've made a choice."

"I know," I say.

"So who truly is the sleeper?" he asks.

"Shut up," I say.

"Do you think you've truly woken?"

"I said shut up."

Within my veins is a dark and viscous feeling, flowing like an oily river into my brain, turning my thoughts to darkness. How quickly sadness wilts into anger.

I go to the kitchen. I stand in the lightless room and dial Richard on the phone. If there's someone to blame for all this. It's him. He was supposed to take care of me. He was supposed to look out for me.

I get a female receptionist who I may or may not have ever spoken to before. I ask for Richard.

"Nobody named Richard works here."

And the emptiness uncoils even more inside me.

"What? What do you mean? Since when?"

"I don't know. I'm new here. I can check and see if we have any information about him."

"Please... I really need to talk to him."

The final threads of desperation are coming undone inside me as I hang waiting for her to offer some resolution to my woes; but whose responsibility is it but my own to resolve my own internal struggles?

Radey's voice sounds from behind me. "I told you. You can't go back. I made sure of it."

"Can I ask who this is?" the woman asks.

I answer. Radey's voice comes out of my own throat like vomit I can no longer hold down. "I am Radey."

I hang up on her.

Chapter 23

Out of the delusioned tomb I'd called home and into the harsh outside light of the early afternoon.

A breath of cool wind washes over me. I scan the wall of suburban homes segregated like patterned cages for cattle down each side of the street I'd lived on—each house surrounded by a moat of fresh-mowed green grass and each with clean cars parked along the drive in front of them. Such is the garden woven for the growth and imprisonment of human minds, but by whose hand was such a field sown?

Regardless of who seeded such a mess, I will set it all ablaze. Slowly but surely. One by one. Each house will be burned to ashen earth, returned to the humble dust from whence it came.

I am the sole savior of those left sleeping soundly under their blankets of delusion—I am the reaper, here to harvest souls of those worthy of my gift and to turn to ash those who aren't. I am the hand of death, and in the nights of deepest darkness, whilst the sleepers are in their deepest comfort, I will come to take from them what they'd never a right to claim.

Pure blue sky overhead. And a scattering of clouds sliding effortlessly across it. My eyes are tender against the beating sun and my heart is empty in its own beating and for a moment I lose my train of thought and I'm not sure what to make of any of this—all these objects beating and pulsing within and without me—all of it brimming pain and separation ceaselessly into a chaotic continuum of life and death.

And when I think further of it I'm not sure what to make of the me that makes of anything. My fleeting thoughts roll like clouds through the clear and present blueness of a sky indifferent—without purpose, and where one fades another rises.

I take a deep breath and shake loose such purposeless ponderings. I focus on the one constant. The faint anger throbbing incessantly in my blood; it is a beacon in the otherwise lightless realm of my awareness. I will follow its incessant flame for I've nothing else to follow.

My car sits parked in the driveway beside me. I reach out my hand and touch the cold steel of its exterior. A mild relief blooms like a budding rose inside me. The vehicle is real and not imagined. I get into it and find the keys and start it, then roll in reverse out of the small driveway and onto the main street. I pull forward and drive for but a few seconds before I notice in my rearview mirror a suspicious dark car parked two houses back. It pulls onto the road and follows close behind me.

Anger, and now paranoia. Symptoms of some condition. Richard could tell me what. But he's not here so they are my new and only friends. Richard can go to hell and burn for eternity for all I care.

I take a right at the first stop sign I come across. I head toward town and sure enough the black car does too. It is, in fact, following me and it doesn't come as a surprise. I wouldn't be surprised if the devil himself were tracing in my wake. After all, is he not lurking behind all of us? Awaiting the weakest of our steps to pounce and overtake us?

I'm not one for shying away from confrontation, devil or not.

There is a large parking lot to my right and I pull into it. The black car slows and pulls in behind me. I want to laugh when I see where we are but I am not in the mood. The building I park in front of is large and made of brown brick. A white cross hangs over the white-painted doors and above the cross a sign hangs in declaration of the nature of the building. It is a Pentecostal church.

The black car parks five spaces away from me to my left. I try to see the driver but the windows are tinted too dark. I get out of my car.

My pursuer's vehicle is an older car, of what type I don't know. But it is clean and shiny and I can see myself and the blue sky behind me reflected on its black exterior. The sight of the car beckons a feeling of familiarity that I can't pinpoint the source of.

And it serves only to enliven my anger.

I walk toward it and I must look like some kind of maniac—my face heaving red—an unshakeable anger throbbing like an awakened volcano behind my eyes. I get within a few steps of the car before its engine revs and it reverses quickly away from me. It shifts into gear then turns around in a hurry, exits the parking lot, and speeds off back the way we came.

I feel like a dog who's just barked away some unworthy predator. I suppose I should be concerned about who they are and what they want but I am not.

The parking lot darkens, going gray beneath a large passing cloud that covers up the sun. I return to my car and sit inside it and contemplate my next move—my next mission. I probe my heart for its truest urging. Then from my pocket I retrieve a billfold, the one I stole from a woman in a toystore days earlier. From within it I take the woman's driver's license. Her photographed face stares back at me like an old friend. Her name is Elizabeth Bathory, and I decide her home is the place I most desire to be.

Elizabeth: If the tides of chance should deem it so, this night may be your last upon this earth.

Chapter 24

I find her house in the early evening in a part of the city I've never been to. I lurk in a small woodland park that has a river running through it. The sound of free-flowing water accompanies the distant chorus of city people and their vehicles. There are lots of trees around me but from where I stand I'm afforded a clean view of Elizabeth's property. I stand watch patiently next to one of the park's largest trees.

Her house sits perched upon an elevated plot of fenced-in land, looming over the sidewalk and the street that runs between her house and the park I'm in. The fencing that separates what she owns and what she does not is made of tall black bars with pointed tips at their tops—the kind of fence you'd find around a graveyard. Two cars sit parked down her driveway near her house. The house is a tall brick building reminiscent of a small castle. The word Victorian comes to mind.

The area of town that surrounds her property is a remnant of a more grandiose and optimistic time. The street that runs past her house also runs past many other buildings of the same castle-like style, most of them filled with shops and restaurants. All of them constructed of the same dark and gray aged brickwork. Each of them once a home for people who thought themselves the rightful kings of reality; each of them now just a crumbling container for the failing businesses within. Each of their pompously constructed barriers to the external world slowly wilting into dust.

While most of the building's original and inherited inhabitants have left town—lost their fortunes or moved to whichever part of the country seemed most suiting to their self-deemed importance—Elizabeth still lives within her castle. She still believes herself worthy of such grandiosity. While indigents starve and die all throughout the world beyond her walls, she thinks it proper that she sits pretty on her elevated plot of land. And I think tonight it may serve her as a deathbed.

I wait until the sun has set and the park I'm in becomes dark enough to serve as a hiding place or escape route if need calls for it. And then I wait longer, until I seldom see pedestrians on any of the concrete walkways that run along the streets; until the drone of cars has become more distant and unthreatening.

Above the hazy glow of the city's lights the night sky is the deepest shade of black, but Elizabeth's house and expansive lawn are well lit by streetlamp and yardlight. There are also many lights lit within her house. They've been on since the setting of darkness and I will not be able to reach her house without being seen if anybody is watching.

But I tell myself I am protected. That my purpose is of the purest type and for it no one will be watching. God, or whatever force dictates reality, will force any witness to turn their eyes from me. For my goal is the same as any god's should be: to bring about awakening to those who've fallen into slumber.

I wait for a lull in the sound of nearby cars and then I cross the street and quickly scale the fence and drop onto her grassy lawn. When my feet touch down I immediately feel like I am on a stage, with the backdrop of the night-veiled city behind me, and her property lights beaming from ahead.

My blood is pure singing electricity, but my movements are slow and calculated. I don't allow myself to feel fazed by such a vulnerable position. There is no chemical supplement for the level of confidence surging within me. If they could package it in pill-form its cost could be greater than that of heroin.

I walk along her house to the back where I find a patch of shade near a window. I stand in the dark and silence and feel what God must feel when he sends an asteroid into Earth; the pure pleasure of a rage about to be released onto something deserving of its wrath.

The room I can see into is dark and large, an unlit bedroom. The light of a hallway is visible through its open doorway directly across from the window.

There are silhouettes of a bed and bedside table. Across the room, near the doorway, a dresser stands with a large mirror sitting atop it. I can almost see down the hallway in the mirror's reflected view.

I take a breath. I close my eyes. Euphoria unfolds, tingling through every cell of me. The world is mine and I've no reason to fear anything in it.

The window is unlocked and slides open without much effort. Oh, Elizabeth. How trusting still you are of the outside world.

You must *want* me to come in.

I crawl through the window, careful not to make a sound. The flooring is hardwood and I make soft, strained steps like a ballerina toward the closet at the opposite end of the room. I can hear a television somewhere, and children talking.

Then there are footsteps which thunder down a stairwell and I pause and listen. They clomp loudly from down the hall and get louder as they approach the doorway of the room I'm in. I know it's Elizabeth. I know it by the force with which she walks; she is punishing the world for being lesser than what she thinks she deserves with each of her steps.

The wood flooring quakes slightly beneath the force of her last few steps before she comes into sight. I have the sudden urge to bolt for the closet but I don't indulge it. I stand my ground in the center of the room. Why would I hide if I've nothing to fear?

Her silhouette shows up in the doorway like an image from a nightmare you can either wish away or confront directly.

And I'm not one to wish away my nightmares.

She freezes. She sees me in the darkness. She glances back the way she'd come, toward the sounds of her children laughing. She looks back to me and says quietly, "Please. Just take whatever you want and leave." She glances back again, then steps slowly into the room saying, "Please. I have kids. Just don't hurt anyone."

I say nothing and don't make a move. She lets out a deep exhalation of relief, the way you exhale when you realize something you had feared was only imagined. She turns on the light and then sucks the dead air of her previous breath right back into her. She clenches like she's about to be submerged in water. The thing she'd imagined is real after all.

I smile and say, "Yes, I'm really here. Now shut the door."

She turns and reaches her arm out to shut it. Her hand is shaking and she pauses for a moment. I imagine she's considering making a run for it, but she thinks better of such an impulse and closes the door, then turns to face me. Her eyes are filled with fear—her body shaking like a brittle blade of grass.

"What do you want?" she squeaks.

"I will take whatever you think you need—whatever defines you." I watch her hyperventilate. "I will take what you hold dearest lest you live a life never knowing how you've wasted it."

"Please. I have kids. Please, just leave."

I think of how she talked to her child on the phone the day prior. "So," I say. "You hold your children most dear, do you? So you'd like that I take them?" I take a step toward her.

She steps backward, putting her back against the door. "No. Please, they're all I have. Nothing else matters. Take anything else."

"Nothing else matters?" I look around the room, at the cleanliness of it and the objects in it. Every article of furniture made from aged dark wood. All of it dustless and glossed with varnish and all of it dimly reflective of the room's dull light. Old, gold ornamental jewelry lying about on the dresser. "None of this stuff—" I gesture with my hands to the room's entirety, "—none of it matters, does it? So why devote your life to it? If it means nothing to you in the end?"

She doesn't seem to comprehend my words. I may as well be speaking another language. Terror has crippled her mind and she is nothing but a frightened, shaking animal, tears running down her cheeks.

Her children burst into laughter down the hall. "It's you or them," I say. "You decide which is more important. Your self, which will continue to exist if you choose it so, or your children, who will continue to exist only if you do not." I step closer to her. Close enough to smell her breath. It smells like popcorn.

She closes her eyes, tries to steady herself. "Just... don't take them."

I reach out my hands and cup her throat within my grip. I feel her blood pulsing beneath my thumbs. Rapid like a bird's beating wings.

And then I squeeze tightly, enough to block the blood and air from flowing and I say, "I will not hurt your children. They are safe. But only if you let me kill you now. Do you understand?"

I think she nods her head but I'm not sure.

"What does it matter if they exist if you're not here to witness them?" I ask. All the while she can't breathe or think, let alone answer me.

Hardly ten seconds pass and she goes limp.

Her body suddenly a bag of lifeless meat only standing for sake of being held up by my grip. And a coldness sets over me, like I've turned a page in the book I've been reading and found it's ended abruptly and has led nowhere—into a void. And then fear pours in to fill the emptiness.

I let go of Elizabeth's throat and her body slumps to the floor. A panic begins to flutter through my mind like a flock of rabid bats. One of Elizabeth's legs is twitching as if an electric shock is passing through her. I am not Radey, I think. I am Cathedra, and oh, dear God, I am insane.

Chapter 25

I'm standing with my back to the room's opened window. A nighttime breeze gently whispers into the room, raising goosebumps in my neck. The impulse to flee is tugging at my nerves. I want to bolt like a frightened animal.

But an animal I am not. I am a human with cinderblocks for feet. I am a human with a conscience that's grown too heavy to let me leave this room.

Freedom is just a leap and a run through darkness away. No one needs to know what I've done. No one needs to know what a horrible, weak person I am. The world of shadows beyond this room offers me hope of escaping any claim to what has happened here. I can run. I can deny.

Still, something is keeping me here. The blackhole-truth of the moment has me in its magnetic grip—my muscles frozen up; my eyes locked in hopeless gaze upon Elizabeth's lifeless body.

This is *my* doing.

And it hurts to know it. It hurts like a fire in my veins.

I turn to face the night and all its shadows. I stare out the window as if staring toward an old friend or a long lost lover. I can skulk away as if this never happened, like a snake in the grass.

But I don't want to escape. I don't want to hide from the truth anymore.

And with that thought, my breathing becomes rapid and shallow. A familiar feeling falling like a curtain over me—sadness, deep and suffocating. I think of Richard, and my desperation to see him—to touch him—is so great it serves to ignite my sadness even further. I weep gasoline, and the painful ache of loneliness envelops me. I feel like I've been set on fire, my every nerve bursting into flames.

I fall to the floor and curl into a fetal position. My sadness expands beyond me. It is the universe. It is all I know. Sadness singing eternally. A convergence of loss, need, and unreciprocated love all erupting into suffering so as to set ablaze the very fabric of reality; the world bearing down on me like a collapsing star.

I choke on my own breath. My lungs constrict and close as if they're breathing smoke.

My vision tunnels into gray, and it blurs more with each painful, pulsing moment of despair unfurling. The world spins and spins and then everything goes black. I pass out.

Chapter 26

Vivid memories flash like seizure-dreams inside my skull.

Fluorescent lighting. A body laid out before me in a room of white. My hands like mechanical tools tending to a graying corpse. Cleaning it. Preparing it. A thick scent permeates the air—the smell of the fluids I use to preserve the body in a presentable state for its mourners to see. A cold, conditioned emptiness keeps my insides numb while I tend to such tasks.

This is a memory I don't want to witness: myself, as an emotionless machine performing programmed tasks upon a human who once lived and loved but does no longer; all the while unaffected and uncaring of the fact that this body once felt joy and pain just as I do. The absence of life within the body mirroring the absence in myself.

I try to separate myself from the emotionless person standing beside the corpse. Whoever they are, I don't want to be behind their eyes, and when I pull away and witness this person from an outward perspective I see that the person is not me but a man dressed in a black suit. At first I think it's Radey but as I look more closely I see this person is actually my father. He notices me observing him and a grin sets across his lips. He shows me his hands and they are covered in blood and I become flushed with terror.

It is an unbearable vision and so I leave it to witness another, one that is more pleasant.

Suddenly I am the child I once was. I'm waking in a bed to my mother's voice. She's saying, "Wake up, Cathedra. It's time for breakfast. I made pancakes, and bacon and eggs. And we've got your favorite—maple syrup." Within her voice is all the warmth and love I could ever need to feel safe in the world.

I open my eyes wide and see her face, her deep blue eyes. Looking into them I can't help but think of swimming in the ocean, of being swept away at sea, but not being scared. I think of being all alone out on the ocean and feeling at peace because the ocean is made of the same thing as her eyes are made of. The color blue.

She ruffles my hair and then leans forward and I feel her body's warmth as she wraps me in her arms and lifts me out of bed. She carries me from my room. In her presence my senses are drenched in raw emotion. Happiness. Love. Bliss. While in her arms, I *know* the world is a good place, and it makes my body tingle with joy. I watch the house as she carries me through it, uncaring and unknowing of how fleeting such contentment is.

She descends a flight of stairs with me still in her arms. She brings me to a dining room with a large window in it. The morning sun is beaming through it and lighting all the dust of the room. She sets me at the big wood table we eat at and I say, "Look, Mom." I point at the dust. It is lit gold and swirling in the air between us.

"Yes," she says. "It's always there. But we're only seeing it now because of how the sunlight is coming through the window."

She points out the window and I try to follow her finger but the sun is too bright. I close my eyes tight. "It's too bright," I say.

I open my eyes and look at her face. Her long blonde hair is messy and funny-looking from having just woken up. I just sit looking at her, feeling like she's the most wonderful person in the world, and I'm the luckiest, for being able to be here with her.

But then I notice something has changed in her face. She's making an expression I've never seen before. She's staring out the window and she doesn't look at me when I say "Mom" to her. Her finger is stuck in the pointing position and she's breathing funny.

I say "Mom" two more times and then I start to feel scared inside.

"Mom!" I shout it at her the way I do sometimes when she won't wake up in the morning, but she still doesn't look at me.

I get more scared, thinking she has turned into a statue or that time has stopped. I get scared thinking I'm all alone in the universe.

I feel the same feeling I felt in the last dream when I saw my father with blood on his hands.

I wake up, happy to leave the dreams behind.

Chapter 27

The familiar dull hum of depression buzzes through my body—it's the lonesome ache of being encaged in meat and skeleton with no one to love or ease the aching. Each day the pressure of the waking world impresses on me a new dawn of pain and separation, but today is different as it is without light, literally.

I open and close my eyelids repeatedly. Still, there is only blackness. A faint earthen scent lingers in the air, a perfume of musk and dust. Somewhere beyond the blindness is the distant and muffled sound of a dog barking.

The animal's fearful song sounds out in a broken repetition. How horrible it must be to be such a creature. Its life spent hypnotized by an unrelenting pendulum of fear and defensiveness—always feeling as if the world is poised against it, some unseen threat forever looming. And so bark it must to fend its fears away.

I try to sit up, but cannot. I try to lift my hands to reach my face, but cannot. Wild panic blooms like wildfire through my nerves, and with it an unwelcome thought enters my mind: that I am entombed somewhere, buried alive.

The sound of children shouting and scuffling about brings my panic to a lull, dispelling the notion of being underground as their excitement is sounding from somewhere nearby. I must be in a house. It is a young boy and girl arguing, or perhaps playing. Either way their quarreling is short-lived, ended abruptly by the sound of a door slamming shut. And then there is silence. The children seem to have left the house and all is quiet and I wonder if I am alone.

I try once again to move with no success. My hands and feet are bound tightly at the wrists and ankles. I'm laid out, Jesus-on-the-cross style, and there is soft cushioning beneath my back. Someone has tied me to a bed.

I wriggle my torso and my upper legs and arms. I flop about uselessly. I try to call out but the same person has seen fit to cover my eyes and seal my mouth.

A pair of high heels knock against a set of stairs then clomp loudly across a wooden floor, growing louder as they grow nearer. My heart spits blood violently through my veins. I feel certain I am moments from being murdered.

Memories of my actions prior to my fainting begin to surface. Cold fear tingles through me as the not-so-obvious becomes painfully obvious: Elizabeth is not dead. She'd only passed out.

A door opens. Then she speaks. "You are mine now."

Her voice is cracked and hoarser than before, like she's been drinking broken glass. Perhaps I damaged her throat.

"I could kill you," she sputters.

I shake the midsection of my body spasmodically; I try to yank my hands and feet free, with no success. My limbs are bound tightly and my panicked movements only serve to cause me pain. I give up and lie still, defeated, my wrists and ankles throbbing.

"Get used to the feeling," she says. "It is the nature of this world." She is quiet, surely looking down at me. I hyperventilate. I've felt panic like this so many times before, but this time the danger is real.

"The world is a den of wolves," she continues. "Wolves upon wolves, in every direction, with no escape. You fill your mouth with blood or you become blood in the mouth of another."

I hear the strained creak of tensing wood coming from near the foot of the bed. The sound of a chair as she sits down upon it.

A long drawn-out sigh pushes from her lungs, and beyond my blindness it is the only noise I hear. My mind drifts, as the minds of those bound, blinded, and gagged tend to do. I imagine I am alone within a lightless cave and the sound of her breath is the wind tumbling in on me from the lighted outside world. For a moment, I imagine she is my redemption. That she is here to lead me into freedom with her grace and forgiveness. But my imaginings quickly fade into the vacuum of reality. She is most likely going to kill me, or at best have me taken off to jail to suffer death of another sort.

When she speaks her voice is jarring, like a bell sounding in the dead of a silent night.

"Someone once told me that the world will always find a way to make a victim of you, if you let your guard down."

She exhales another forceful, agonized sigh. The sigh of an angry mother for a disobedient child. I imagine her rolling her eyes.

"My dearest insane person...." Apparently this is her chosen name for me. "Never let yourself forget that if you let yourself be gentle toward the world then the world will treat you as such and it will wilt you without a thought."

My fear is beginning to give way to anger. I want to shout at her that this is not true, that I've seen the vicious way she speaks to her children and that it is wrong of her. I want to tell her that she is the victim, not me; that I only wanted to wake her from the lies she tells herself. But I am unable to speak so I can't tell her anything. I can only listen to her ramble on about the world, with no way to contend or to convince her of her wrongness. And for it her voice is truth and I am merely the silence into which the truth is spoken.

She stamps her foot loudly against the floor, as if to

interrupt my thinking, and my entire body gets damp; a cold sweat soaking through my clothing. "God's way is the way of terror." Her voice is loud and ominous; the voice of someone preaching gospel to a church of sinners. "Fear is the heartbeat that keeps his world alive. And kept alive it is only so He can bear witness to the suffering."

The floor creaks. Her high heels knock slowly across it. Her steps cease and she speaks again.

"You must be tough as a mountain to survive—as cold as steel; more violent than violence if you want to thrive in this world where every living thing is out to feed upon the next."

Her voice is coming from my right side and I imagine she is staring contemplatively out a window, down from her castle-home at the world of lesser beings.

"What happened last night.... It will not happen again. For the sake of my children's safety, and mine. I will never be soft again."

I hear a loud clicking noise and then the sound of traffic pours into the room. She's opened a window.

A nauseating quietness fills the room, while the sound of cars buzz past in the world beyond it. I wonder if Elizabeth is planning to jump from the window. Or if she's planning to throw me from it. Elizabeth's voice has become my only anchor to the external world and I find myself desperately wishing for her to speak again.

And when she does it startles me. Her voice is inches from my face. The heat and moisture of her breath flow over my skin.

"You are but a sleeping lamb in a dream of hungry shadows," she whispers. "And you are mine now. And I can do to you whatever I desire."

Chapter 28

The seconds are days and the minutes are months and the hours drag on so long they outstretch any scale of time.

In my eyes: a void of formless dark. In my ears: the empty quietude of a stranger's lifeless home. Elizabeth has left me alone here with no way to escape, tethered to a bed as a means to an end of only her knowing. Where she's gone, I can only wonder.

Every heartbeat is agony. Every breath followed by the pain and regret of having taken it.

All I've got to keep me company is the tortured landscape of my own inner thoughts. I've no control over the external world and no hope for any future of my choosing. I wait and toil at taunting thoughts—of my impending imprisonment, of the looming possibility of being murdered.

I think this is the torture Elizabeth intended.

At this point, I want it to all be over, by whatever means required.

The question that keeps repeating inside me is:

Why am I here? Why did this happen?

I ask it like a dog barking into darkness. An answer never comes—not from myself or God or any other voice.

The question is quicksand—a darkness I sink into—and I keep sinking until my mind is blacked out by hopelessness entirely, until there is no voice to pose the question, and no reason to pose it in the first place; until there is nothing but silence inside me—blessed silence. I find reprieve in the absence of any hope or grasping thought. In it, I find surrender, absolute and wonderful.

There is nothing to fear when there is nothing to fear it; there is nothing outside the self when there is nothing within to resist against it. I feel empty—blissfully empty.

If my lips weren't sealed so stiffly I'd be smiling.

Chapter 29

The moment can never hurt you once you've given up on pursuing something beyond it. Surrender, and you'll find freedom from the pains that plague you, whether they're real or imagined.

My body may be imprisoned, blinded, and alone within an empty room, but that doesn't mean I have to be. I am free to let go of it all, and let go I do.

It feels like falling from the edge of the world, with nothing beneath to catch me.

Under the darkness of my despair—and beneath my panicked mind—I fall until I find a lightness untouched by suffering, and in it coiled I find a vision imbued with all its lightness, or perhaps it is a dream.

I think I may have drifted into sleep because I am suddenly a child standing barefooted in a wet and grassy lawn under a night sky. A light mist rolls across my view, and beyond the mist is a large, white, two-storied house. It is the home where I spent my youngest years. It is the house I loved my parents in. And within the house I feel my mother's presence, awaiting me, her arms surely open to take me in.

I run toward the house. I run toward my home.

This is the place I've sought so hard to forget and never remember. But why would I seek to erase a place so peaceful, so wonderful and inviting? A place so full of love?

There's that question again. Why?

With the question posed, a cold terror grips me. Tears stream from my eyes. Because I remember my mother is not in the house, not anymore. The grass underfoot and all around me morphs into a million snakes, their tendrilled tongues all outstretched and flickering. I look to my feet to see the wetness upon them is not from water but from blood.

A noise within the room wakes me from the visions. A gentle rapping; the sound of a bird or squirrel pecking or picking at the glass of the window near the bed I'm bound to. It is there and then it's gone.

And I'm back in my private darkness. Confined. My breath the only sound.

Then there is a deafening crash so loud my heart stops beating and my lungs lock shut. There is a whoosh of air and the sounds of traffic flow through the room. Someone has broken the window open.

Has Elizabeth been in here with me the entire time, watching over me? Contemplating what to do with me?

Oh dear God. I don't want to die. Not like this. I think of the snakes in my dream, their fangs dripping wet with venom; unavoidable, poised to strike and steal my life.

"Cathedra?"

It's the voice of a man. His voice like warm velvet, soft and familiar as it trickles into my ears. It sends a warm shockwave-shiver down my spine. Tears spurt from my eyes and I shake my torso up and down excitedly.

"Hold on, I'll get you out of here."

It's the voice of my savior. It's Richard.

"Just stay calm. It's okay."

A world of light pours into my eyes, and with it, Richard's silhouetted body is standing over me. Around him, glaring, is a soup of out-of-focus form and color. The room is lit bright by the burning light of the evening sun beaming through the window.

I am breathless.

Golden clouds of dust are spiraling through the air of the room, rolling over us as they're carried in the gentle evening breeze. The beauty of this moment outshines that which is bearing witness to it. I am in awe. In my entire life, thoughts have never felt more redundant; they fall away like dead leaves.

The colors of the world have never looked so lovely and my blood has never felt so hot inside my veins. I am mesmerized at the beauty of this moment, and the beauty of Richard. At least, I think it's Richard.

I strain my eyes to make more clear the sight of him. His head is shaven, and despite my knowing it is him, his appearance and demeanor is altogether unfamiliar.

He removes the tape from my mouth, which makes my lips feel tender against the air. I can't find words to speak. He unties my hands. Once my arms are free to move I sit up and pull him close to me and hold him tight, like he is a life raft and if I let go I'll sink to the bottom of the ocean and never see light again. I can feel his heartbeat pulsing through our clothing. It is the rhythm of my own heart. It is all that matters to me right now. I feel love for him.

"Your hair," I whimper. "What did you do to your hair? You look like an alien." I say these words and then I begin to laugh uncontrollably, while tears stream from my eyes and slide down my cheeks.

"After what happened... I figured it was time for a new beginning," he says. "And also, the fire burned most of it off."

This makes me cry even harder. "I'm sorry. I'm so sorry." My voice comes out thick with snot and spit. I don't know where the words are coming from or why they're coming out of me, but I can't stop them. "Oh dear God, I'm so sorry. I'm so sorry, Richard."

"It's okay. It's okay. We need to get you out of here." He pulls away from me and goes to the foot of the bed. "I'm not sure how much time we have, but I'd rather not be here when she gets back." He unties my feet.

"You mean Elizabeth? Do you... know her?" My voice is meek and cracked, vulnerable. I am emotionally exposed and for the first time in a long while I'm not trying to hide it from him. And why would I want to show him otherwise? The feel of tears upon my face is comforting; it means I'm the one hurting and I'm not hurting someone else.

"Yes, I know her, or, I did," he says. "There are only so many crazy people in this city." I think he's trying to make a joke but its punchline is lost on me. He takes notice and elaborates. "She was a patient of mine, like you."

There is a small voice at the back of my mind, thinking: And just like me, you left her a total depraved mess. But I stay silent and a feeling of sadness wells up in replacement of the thought. The sadness grows into an empathy, and I begin to cry for Elizabeth. She *is* just like me—afraid, in pain, and looking for someone to lead her to a life better than what the world has shown her. And Richard has been doing his best in a losing battle for the both of us. I cry for him as well.

I scoot off the bed and stand up next to Richard. My legs feel weak and they nearly buckle under my weight. Richard holds me while I steady myself and when I feel more sure-footed he begins leading me toward the broken-open window, toward the raw light of the late-day sun which is emanating from beyond it.

Relief is coursing wildly in my veins. I feel like a queen being returned her riches after having them stolen from me, yet what is being returned to me is nothing more than the world in all its normalcy, as it always has been, yet shown in new light for all the pain I've suffered.

With Richard at my side I take slow steps toward that normalcy and say, "I thought I was going to die."

"You still just might, my darling."

Sounding out loudly from behind us is the voice of a woman; the voice of a bad dream come to life.

We turn to see Elizabeth standing in the doorway to the room. She's clothed all in black, in a dress likely made for attending funerals. She looks much like a ghost you'd expect to find haunting a house such as the one we're in—her skin faded pale, her eyes shadowed and empty of love.

"Richard... I don't know what brought you here, but whatever the reason," she hisses, "you must know that you cannot take her. She tried to kill me and I deserve this. I've earned it. She is mine."

Richard is not shaken by her words, not even slightly. He answers back, as my brave protector, with force and certainty.

"You will let us go, or I will call the police and tell them everything you've ever told me. I will show them what's in your basement."

My mind reels at the thought of what he's referring to, but I can see on Elizabeth's face that her heart has skipped a beat at its mention.

She plays her best poker face and says solemnly, "You are an accomplice."

"I most certainly am not," Richard says.

"You will be held accountable," she contends. "And you know it. All that I've done... you let it happen under your watch."

"What you did was of your own choosing. My only goal was to guide you to seeing the truth of your actions, so that you would not repeat them—so that you could change," he says. "This—right now—is your chance to show you've changed."

"People never change," she says. "The ways of the world never change, and this—right here—is proof of that."

Richard breathes deeply before speaking his next words. "If I must suffer for how I dealt with your... situation, then so be it. I'm prepared to accept that."

He turns slowly from her, and prompts me to do the same. We take a few slow steps toward the window and just as the world outside is within arm's reach, Elizabeth's horse-hoof footsteps begin clomping loudly behind us, getting louder as she quickly picks up pace in our direction.

In response, Richard spins himself around quickly and pushes me out of Elizabeth's path. I lose my balance and fall, first hitting the bed softly, then tumbling to the hardwood floor.

Elizabeth roars with a loud, guttural wailing sound as she charges haphazardly toward Richard. Still in high heels, she wobbles like a robot making its first attempt at running. Yet she runs fast enough that the distance of the room is crossed in the pulsing of a moment. Richard stands his ground stoically, like a man who is about to meet his unavoidable demise, without a hint of fear behind his eyes.

Elizabeth connects with him, and clamps her arms around him as a football player would, but instead of tackling him to the ground or attacking him, she embraces him in the most violent and awkward hug I've ever witnessed. Her body squirms and convulses—she writhes and slinks to the floor, where she continues hugging his legs and sobbing.

She clings to him like a mother would her dead child, letting out a dissonant string of shrieks and weepings—a melody of unconsolable despair.

Richard seems unfazed. He places his hand upon her hand, perhaps to comfort her.

Something truly has changed in him.

Minutes pass before her sobs fade and become a dry whimper, and then Richard helps her up and leads her to the bed and she lays herself gently upon it.

"I knew this day would come," she says, as she curls into a fetal position. She is shivering and Richard takes the bed's white sheeting and covers her in it. "The mouth of God is closing in on me," she says painfully. "And there's nothing I can do to stop its closing... nothing I can do but just... surrender."

She draws a long, deep breath, the sort someone takes

before diving underwater, and then she becomes quiet. I can see her body is gently breathing beneath the blankets. I think she's fallen into sleep.

I rise from the floor quietly, and then Richard and I make our way through the broken window to the world outside, leaving Elizabeth to her dreams.

Chapter 30

The city outside Elizabeth's house is alive and vibrant, pulsing. Everything is gold and beautiful, painted softly in the ebb of twilight glow. Distant buildings stand ominous and silhouetted and glistening in the sinking sun's orange light. There are multitudes of people passing by on a nearby sidewalk, beyond the fence that surrounds her property.

I find it so strange to think the world continued while I lay thinking my life was nearing its end. Actually, I find it comforting—to know the world's heart would have kept on beating even if mine had not.

Richard takes my hand and leads me away from the house. I look back and see that I'd been imprisoned in the same room I'd snuck into, the night prior. Richard continues leading me as if I am a person in shock who cannot lead themselves. My senses are those of a newborn fawn, clumsy and slow to adjust to the external world.

He leads me to the tall graveyard-like fence. He asks me if I can climb it and I say that I think I can. We scale the fence and drop to the ground outside it. I take one last look at the house that had been my home for a day. I imagine the house as a tombstone, and that part of me died inside it. Richard tugs my hand and leads me down the street to his car.

Once again, the not-so-obvious becomes painfully obvious. Richard's car is the black car that had followed me. He'd been waiting for me at my house, and then he tracked me after I left. I wonder if he witnessed what I'd done to Elizabeth.

He sees the look on my face and says, "I couldn't have imagined anything like this would happen—that, of all places, you'd come here." He pauses and says, "I needed to see what would happen."

These words hurt me—dredging up old feelings of being a helpless victim in a meaningless experiment, poked and prodded by an uncaring overseer.

However, when I look into Richard's eyes, I can see he is not uncaring. He cares deeply about me. I tell myself no good will come of becoming suspicious of him. I push the darkness from my mind.

I get into the car with him and we drive off, leaving Elizabeth's house to disappear in the rearview mirror. As we drive, any uneasiness brought on by his words gives way to a warm gratitude. I'm glad to be alive, and I'm glad to be with Richard.

Chapter 31

I am quiet as we drive.

I watch all the humans as we pass them. Some of them are in cars, others walk along the street. All of them are individually luminous and interesting in a way I've never witnessed before, each lit by the evening sun and each lit also by something deeper and more difficult to explain. Every one of them, without exception, the hapless victims of their own implanted suffering, just like me. All of them host to unmet hopes and desires; all of them host to their own personally tailored memories of love gained and lost. But still they all keep trying for something better, and still they all keep sharing love amongst themselves. This is why they shine and this is where we differ.

My heart swells and burns inside me.

"Is this what it feels like to be normal?" I ask out loud while looking out the window. "Everything seems... really intense, and interesting."

I see a woman carrying a small child. She stands with the

helpless boy cradled in her arms at a busy street corner waiting for the streetlight to change so they can cross. I can see how much she loves her child and it makes me feel loved. It feels wonderful. I turn to look at Richard. His brow is scrunched.

"Huh?" He is distracted, deep in his own thoughts.

I decide the answer is irrelevant.

"What were you talking about back there?" I ask.

"When?"

"At Elizabeth's, you said something about telling the police about things she'd told you, and showing them what was in her basement."

I can tell he doesn't want to answer. It takes him nearly a minute to respond.

"She's done things which were... very destructive, to herself and others. And she's kept these things hidden from most everyone, and for a while she even kept them hidden from herself, which made matters even worse. That's where I came in. I helped her to see who she really was."

My palms are getting sweaty and I suddenly really want to get out of the car. I don't want to hear him talk anymore, because there's a tone to his voice which makes me think he's going to turn this on me somehow. An urge to hurt something is rapidly growing inside me.

Richard notices. He looks to me and something changes in his face. The tenseness in his brow dissipates, falls away, like a glacier slipping from a shelf of stone into water.

"It is in the past now. She's found a way to care for herself and her family. Things can always change," he says.

There is a wet glaze over his eyes, and a softness behind his stare that I don't think I've ever seen before. I find it impossible to stay mad at him.

"Has something changed in you?" he asks.

"I think so," I say. "I don't feel mad."

"Really? Just like that? It's just gone?"

"Well, it's not that I don't still have it, it's just that... I feel something else too, something better."

"What?"

"I don't know what to call it. I've never felt it before." I look out my window. In the distance there are purple rain clouds dripping wetly down the dome of dusky orange sky. "Is acceptance a feeling? I'm just... okay with the way things are. Everything is just... happening, and I'm okay with it."

I close my eyes. I imagine myself drifting effortlessly down a river, through a darkened forest. I smile and say, "I feel free."

Chapter 32

It occurs to me Richard is up to something and when I ask him what that something is he takes an uncomfortable moment to contemplate how to respond, like a chess player considering his next move.

He opens his mouth to speak, then closes it. Then he tells me, simply, that it's time for me to see something and it's important that I see it tonight while I'm still raw from my traumatic experience. When I ask him to elaborate, he tells me to just wait, and to trust him. And despite the oddness of this all, I do. He drives us out of town without another word.

And so the sky goes dark. We drive through forests darker than the dying twilight, past hills and fields and empty nature unbuilt upon by humans. Miles and minutes, stacked on miles and minutes, until we're far enough from town that the city-glow is entirely vanished behind us, and we've only nature and darkness peering in on us from the outside world.

The car hums and shakes over a remote, winding road. The

pavement is cracked and bumpy. I ask again where we're going and Richard says, "You'll see. Don't worry, we're almost there." I look out my window. The tall grass of the surrounding fields is well lit. Above us, hanging like some ghostly spotlight, a yellowed full moon paints the shadowed world in blue and gray.

I scan the distant horizon. The forests afar look black and above the blackened trees is a deep blue sky and higher still are white dots glistening, the source of their light unfathomably far away, in both distance and time.

"So long ago nothing can remember them," I say out loud.

"Huh?" Richard says.

"Nothing."

So incredibly small I am amidst the scope of the outward universe, and so undeserved is the sense of safety unfolding within myself. I peel my eyes from the starry sky and look to Richard. I feel gratitude.

A drip of warm water tickles the bare skin of the hand I've left resting on my lap. A tear fallen from my cheek. I look back out my window. I feel contentment so boundless I can't help but think it'd be okay if I were to die right now.

"There's no suffering, and no pain or fear, when I just witness the moment unfolding for what it is—when I just *see* the world around me, luminous and glistening, without resistance to it."

Richard hears my words and reaches across my lap to

clasp my hand with his.

Out in the dark—in the deep shadowy blue. Across the fields. Beneath the glowing moon. A tall white house comes into view, standing lone amidst the soft swaying fields. It is large and two-storied. I see one road leading to it and in the yard surrounding it I see a large solitary tree with branches like shadowy snakes winding upward through the air in a futile attempt to breach the lighted moon.

"Wait... I know this place." My voice slips out of me without me wanting it to. I stare hard at the lone tree at the end of the long road to our right. Its branches are enormous, the kind a child would build a tree fort on. However the tree looks to be dying or is dead already; no leaves, just a skeletal frame of barren branches.

"Yes. It's where you grew up," Richard says. And he slows the car and turns onto the road that leads to the house.

As the car rolls off the paved road and onto the rough dirt and stone of the driveway, a high-pitched clinking noise startles us both. Something has struck the front window. I notice a small crack in the glass forming directly in front of me; a spider web of lines unfurling from the fracture point.

"What the hell?" Richard is straining his eyes, trying to make sense of the break in the glass.

"Must've been a rock kicked up by the tires?" I say.

"That doesn't make sense," he says. His brow is scrunched

as he tries to wrap his mind around it.

He slows the car then stops and gets out. So I get out too. We stand looking at the window. And then Richard looks to our surroundings for answers, but finds none. Nothing but tall grass in every direction.

"It's just so weird," he says. "That the glass would just break like that. It's like someone threw a rock at us."

"But who would do that?" I ask. I turn from the car and look down the road to the building that once was my home. It's perhaps half a mile away. The dark house stands as an impersonal sight. Looking at it is like looking at a photograph of a distant and unmet relative. You know there's a connection between yourself and what you're looking at, but only because someone else explained it to you.

"I don't know," Richard answers back. "You didn't see anyone, did you?"

"What? Are you serious? You think someone is out there? Like, watching us? Right now?"

I think of Radey and I feel fear.

Then in my mind a memory begins to unravel, sparked by the notion of Radey being out there somewhere, watching us.

It is a memory of Radey. I see him sitting beneath a lone tree in a field like this one. He's watching a house like this one also. The tree is slightly different in the memory—smaller, not as sturdy. And there is a barn in the yard of the house in the memory, but otherwise it looks much the same. Even moreso once Radey sets the barn on fire and it burns to the ground. As if he were molding that moment to match this one. He sat and watched the barn burn and he felt freedom at the sight of its destruction.

I look toward my childhood home and imagine setting fire to it. I feel something welling up in me—perhaps a sense of freedom—at the thought of it.

A voice that is not Richard's startles me.

"You are here only because I have willed it so."

It is Radey, his voice sounding out from somewhere in the darkness.

"Your freedom is as inevitable as that of any other subject trapped within an object."

His voice is a whisper in the air, from what direction I'm not sure.

"I will set you free."

I look around at the wind-swept fields and distant treelines. I turn and see Richard. He is oblivious, picking at the small crack in the windshield.

"It's getting bigger," he says.

Richard didn't hear Radey's voice, and it means I am going crazy, but I find this fact relieving, because if it weren't the case then Radey would be real and nothing would be more terrifying than that.

"What do you mean?" I ask.

"The crack is getting bigger, it's spreading. Look."

I walk to him and stand beside him and look at the glass. The spider web of lines has expanded to cover nearly half the windshield. The shattering is slowly overtaking the glass entirely. Driving will be troublesome for Richard when we leave.

I turn around and stare toward the house and I could swear I catch a glimpse of a shadowy figure moving about near the house's door. It is a vague blob of darker shadow amidst many shadows. It drifts quickly along the front of the house and then disappears around the far corner. It may have been a person, or it may have been imagined.

"Hey, Richard. Does anyone live here now?"

"No. Nobody lives here." Richard sounds slightly irritated, like a father tinkering with a car's engine in a garage who's just been distracted by a child. He is staring futilely at the slowly breaking pane of glass, helpless to stop its disintegration.

He exhales deeply, defeated. It seems he's surrendering to the fact he has no power over the object before him. And then he says something that completely stops my breathing.

"I know it was you that burned my house down."

He looks at me, and I at him, both in silence. I think he's waiting for me to respond but I've no words. The memory has surfaced inside me and it's undeniable. I fight the urge to tell him that it wasn't me, that it was Radey.

After a long, breathless moment filled only by the noises of nature—of distant bugs chirping and the pulsing song of wind—he says, "I could have very well died. I lost everything I owned. I should hate you, but I don't. I have nothing, so I've nothing worth hating for."

"I have nothing, and I hate the world all the more for it," I say.

"So why did you do it? Did you want me to die?"

"I don't know. In the moment that I set your house on fire it was like you didn't exist anyway. You were just a troublesome... thing. You were just a *thing* that was a source of pain for me and I guess I wanted you gone, yes."

"And now?"

"Now I know I have nothing to gain from casting blame on anything else. I carried that impulse far enough, and gained nothing from it but more of what I was trying to avoid. My life is filled with pain, and loss, and I'm not sure I even know how to love anymore. What I did to you... what I did to Elizabeth... it is so far beyond something I can have a reason for. I know I need help."

Once again there is no speaking between us, just the two of us staring at one another amidst the song of drifting wind and undulating bug noises. And when I speak, my words, however gentle, shoot through the static of nature like a siren. "I just want to find some sort of genuine peace for myself." I feel my cheeks get wet with tears. I wipe them away.

"I'm not sure that's a possibility, for anyone," he says.

I turn away from him and begin walking toward the house.

Richard starts to follow me but I turn around and ask him not to.

I tell him I need some time to look around by myself. I ask him if that's okay. He is apprehensive but he says that, yes, that's okay and that he'll be here if I need him.

And so I head for the house alone, hoping to chase down the shadowy figure I may or may not have witnessed moments ago.

Perhaps it was a ghost. A ghost with answers.

As I'm walking I realize I want to find Radey. I want to witness him as something separate from myself, one last time.

"The truth of who we are lies behind the veil of what we are most afraid of." These words play like a song repeated in my head.

Chapter 33

I am approaching the forgotten home of my childhood. And I am lost in thought, thinking:

Nothing in this world hurts more than love.

Love is the uncontrolled fire born beside us in our mother's womb. We are doomed to love and lose something—anything, everything—in this world. And it's the losing of what we love most that becomes the very fabric of our identity. To be alive is to gain and then let go of something greater than the sum of its parts. It is the loss of something that gave purpose to the otherwise meaningless and mangled universe—it is the loss of such a wondrous thing that can never again be recovered that defines us most as living creatures.

Who then are the lucky ones? Those who find release in death or those left to bear the burden of their loss? Perhaps, at the end of a life long-lived and stained deeply by loss and suffering, death is the greatest of God's kindnesses. In it, we find release—total and final—and are met as one with all we've lost.

We gain then lose then regain again.

These thoughts gently course within my skull, like some graveyard serenade whispered softly from the lips of the great beyond. Worded emanations, each, of a feeling that is all too often all too easy to hide from. It is death's faint and aching whisper, silent and subtle, calling out from behind the beating of my blood. Aching. Pulsing. Longing. Sending chills into my bones and slowing my steps as I approach the tall white house before me; the house that housed my childhood, the house that hides my memories.

My body is telling me to stop—to turn away. My insides feel brittle and vulnerable. I am a defenseless child carelessly creeping toward a den of sleeping demons. My confidence of mere minutes ago is crumbling and now my legs are weak and stumbling. Every ounce of me is screaming for me to stop but I don't heed the impulse. I feel careless. I feel brave. I bear down and brace for whatever painful memories are housed within the white walls of the building before me.

The house is just an object, I tell myself—just a lifeless frame of wood and other building materials—nothing to be afraid of.

On a small stoop of steps that lead to the front door I find Radey sitting, perched like a blackbird in the pale moonlight. The sight of him is so different now—now that I know he's not real—now that I'm no longer afraid of him.

He rises to his feet as I approach and speaks out in a voice deep and ominous—a rumble. It stops me in my tracks. I swear I feel the earth trembling underneath me; his voice, as always, a beacon for the collapsing of my reality.

"Every part will be unseated by the whole; every mind is but a whisper in white noise. I am that white noise. Do you know who I am?"

His lips curve into a smile and suddenly I'm not so sure anymore. Suddenly I am afraid. His voice sounds too real and too alien to be a mere projection of my own mind.

"I've seen worlds come and go," he says, speaking in a breathy whisper. "I've seen suns collapsed—turned into nothingness. I've seen black holes... universes born. I've seen all things come and go and I will still be here when you are gone."

His voice carries in the wind as if it is the wind itself. My legs are trembling and I feel faint. I've made a terrible mistake.

He begins laughing maniacally and behind his eyes I see an absolute void of light and life. I see death in him, and I see that I am nothing to him. I am disposable.

"You cannot run from me," he says, "for I *am* you, but you are not me."

"But..." I'm finding it impossible to speak in his presence. My words choke on themselves. My tongue is a cold, lifeless worm clogging up my throat.

"But what?" He smiles again. "Did you think I was but

another of your delusions?" This sends him laughing, roaring with laughter. "I am the arc of time upon which you break yourself. I am of greater realness than you can even fathom." His laughter grows loud as thunder—a noise to deafen me to all other noises. "I am the fire born beside the birth of all things. By my light, you shall see the world for what it is."

His laughter goes dead and he stares into me like a lion about to pounce upon its prey. I try to run but my legs won't listen. I'm frozen, like a stupid animal unworthy of its own survival.

"I will pluck your eyes from the mind that feeds them fear." His final words.

What happens next is like a dream.

The deep black color of his suit begins to spill out from the boundaries of his clothing, infecting the air around him like a cloud of spilled ink. And quickly his body becomes veiled entirely by the murky darkness. I can no longer tell where he begins and ends or where he even is. It's as if he was only a reflection in a pool of water that someone has thrown a stone into.

For a moment I think he's vanished. For a moment I feel safer knowing he's not real.

But I am wrong. Dead wrong. I stop breathing when I see what is truly happening. He is changing, shifting form, becoming something else altogether.

As my eyes adjust I see that what I'm staring at is not a

cloud of darkness but a tuft of black feathers—the breast plumage of some enormous shadowy bird. I look upward and see it looming over me. A giant raven larger than any human, with blood-red orbs for eyes and a beak the size of a human arm, sharp and glistening like a black scythe blade in the moonlight, surely poised to pierce my guts and eat my innards should I make one wrong move.

I kneel slowly to the ground, keeping my eyes locked on the face of the creature. Its deep sunken eyes are watching me with a terrifying indifference. Behind its gaze I sense the presence of something dreadful and familiar. I feel suddenly the ghosts of my parents coursing in my veins. Some painful memory being tugged out from my subconscious by the sight of this creature.

In my mind's eye I see my mother's face as she stares out a window at something I've willed myself to long since forget. She's in the dining room of the house I grew up in. I am a child seated at a table beside her.

As I'm on the verge of fully remembering whatever it was that caught my mother's eye, the monstrous bird before me fluffs its feathers and spreads its wings and I'm pulled back to the terror of the moment at hand.

Like a kite that's caught the wind, the creature's full wingspan is spread out in the air before me. It flaps its feathered breadth in such a threatening way that I'm certain my life is about to end. Eclipsed by the creature's body is the blue-lit starry sky;

eclipsed is any hope for escape.

Gusting breaths of wind pulse against my skin with each flap of wings and I'm fumbling with my hands across the dirt and grass around my feet, searching for something to defend myself with. The creature watches me as any bird would, as if I am only an object of curiosity, as if it has no understanding of the subjectivity behind my every movement. As if it may, at any moment, decide to find out what I taste like.

My blind fingers touch upon something cold and sharp, a shard of glass. I clasp onto it and rise quickly to my feet. I hold it out like a magic wand toward the creature. The creature is unimpressed. It stares dumbly at me, like I'm an ant that's raised some feeble tool to defend itself.

The fate of an ant in a bird's belly is not one I'd like to suffer through. I turn and run for Richard.

I've no feeling in my legs and I have to look down to be sure I'm actually running. All I can do is pray my flopping limbs continue to carry me forward without tangling up in themselves.

As I'm running I hear deep whooshing breaths of wind—an intermittent gust of cool air pressing down on me, emanating from somewhere just above and behind me. It feels as though I'm trying hopelessly to outrun a tornado. I brace myself for the feeling of talons piercing my body and tearing me to shreds.

But it doesn't come, and I'm afraid the anticipation will kill me before it does.

Richard is but a few breaths away, close enough he can surely see what is happening to me. He is standing casually next to the car but stiffens as I draw near.

"What is it? What's the matter?" His voice is calm but concerned.

I try to answer back but can't find my voice. Once I'm near enough to see the features of his face, I stop running. I listen to myself breathing and am surprised by the quietude all around us. The noises which had been pursuing me just moments ago are gone. Between us, just the sounds of nature, and my lungs heaving.

"Cathedra. What is it? What's the matter? You're shaking." He steps close to me and puts his hands onto my shoulders.

"I... don't know." My voice cracks. "I think I may be insane."

Chapter 34

"You are not crazy." Richard's voice warms me like a blanket. He pulls me close. He hugs me.

"I tried to kill you." My face is pressed into his shirt. A puddle of tears forming in the fabric.

"But you didn't kill me," he says. "You set me free."

I pull back from him and wipe the tears from my face. I stare at him in disbelief. I know what he said. I just can't believe he said it.

He takes a deep breath before he continues. His calm demeanor crumbles and his words spill out in a way I'm not accustomed to. He talks like I do when I'm hurting so bad my words can hardly hold together.

"My whole life had become nothing." His voice is shaking. "Every day was just a hopeless routine, cyclical and meaningless. I'd become a ghost haunting my own life, forever a victim to what had happened in my past."

His face is darkened but I can see tears running down his cheeks, the wetness glimmering faintly in the moonlight.

"You didn't take my life," he continues. "The only things you took from me were the objects that imprisoned me. All I've lost is a home that housed my own complacency. Cathedra..." He puts his hands back onto my shoulders. He looks straight into my eyes. He looks so intensely into me I feel it like a fire in my heart. "Cathedra. I have never been happier in my entire life. I have nothing to lose. I am absolutely free."

There are no words to describe how this makes me feel. I feel a whirlwind of emotions, all at full intensity: regret, fear, sadness, and joy. Perhaps it's the joy I'm most afraid of. I feel proud of what I did and this terrifies me.

His face stiffens and he looks at me as if about to deliver grave news. "I brought you here with the hope that you could confront your own past, and finally let it go and move past it. I want to return the favor. I want to set you free."

His hands slide down my sides and he clasps my hands in his. The heat of his blood meeting with the heat of mine makes me feel not so alone. It makes me feel loved. And with such a feeling comes a memory. A painful memory of a time when such a feeling was a constant. A memory of my mother forms vividly within me.

"I remember, she woke me up and—" My throat is trembling. I take a moment to swallow hard, to try and steady my breathing. "She made pancakes and I—and I..."

"Who did? Your mother? What are you saying?"

"Yes... my mother. She was... her eyes were made of ocean and... my father... I... he...." Within my mind, a fuse that shorted out long ago has just been reconnected; a memory comes flooding down the wire. "My dad's name was Radey?"

"Yes. Do you remember anything else?"

"Yes... I remember that morning. I was just sitting there. I was happy... and I just sat there. I didn't know what was going on."

"Think back Cathedra, think hard. I'm here for you. It's okay. What happened that morning?"

"Mom... she saw something outside. It scared her."

"What was it? What did she see?" He squeezes my hands gently as he asks this. I get the feeling he knows the answer and it is not a pleasant one.

"He was..."

I feel so weak it's as if I'm deep underwater and the pressure of the world is about to crush me. The sadness is unbearable.

"Cathedra. It's okay." He moves close and tries to hug me but I pull back. My emotions, as always, are a fragile bird, scared away by his closeness. Coldness overtakes me.

"I don't want to do this," I say.

Radey is standing behind me. I feel his breath as he whispers in my ear. His words come out my mouth as if they are my own.

"Your love means nothing to me," I say to Richard, as if

these are the perfect words to hurt him. "You used me as an object and I only treated you the same when I lit your house on fire."

I see fear on Richard's face. He's trying to figure out what has come over me. Behind me, Radey is breathing deep, excited breaths.

"You are afraid of what you cannot control." I laugh wickedly and then say, "And you should be. The world doesn't care for you in the slightest. It will destroy everything you love and then it will destroy you as well. You'll be all alone in death save for the pain of all you've lost to keep you company. Your life is meaningless."

"Cathedra," he says, trying to keep his calm. "Yes, everything dies. And it's terrible, and painful, but it's not without purpose. It's only meaningless if there's no love shared between those of us still living. Love gives loss meaning."

This sends me into a fit of laughter. Tears stream from my eyes and suddenly I'm weeping. "You are nothing to me." My voice is meek and feeble; my words a failing dam for all my sorrow.

"You don't mean that. I know you don't." He takes a step toward me.

"Yes... I do." My final lie before I surrender to the truth. He *is* something to me; he is *everything* to me. I stumble toward him.

He embraces me, and I him.

With me in his arms he says, "I love you, so much."

"I love you too," I say. "And I can't lose you. I won't ever lose you."

He makes a grunting sound like an animal and his body jerks in one quick spasm. It startles me and I step back from him.

"No... no, no, no." My voice spills out in a feverish panic.

Radey is standing behind Richard. His hand is at Richard's side. It is hard to see but there is blood. Lots of blood. A black puddle pooling in the dirt by Richard's feet. Radey has stabbed him, his hand is clasped tightly to a blade plunged deep in Richard's abdomen.

Richard holds his hands to the wound, he touches his fingers upon Radey's hands as if to make sure that they are real.

His eyes are the panicked eyes of a dying animal.

"Richard?" I squeak.

Radey pulls his hand from Richard's side. There are spurts of blood. I can't breathe and in a heartbeat the blade is at Richard's throat.

"How does it feel to be just a... *thing*? Just a thing that dies?" Radey hisses into Richard's ear.

"Better than it does to be a thing that believes it doesn't." Richard struggles to choke out each word as Radey holds the blade against his Adam's apple. He speaks to Radey as if he's spoken with him before.

"What is that supposed to mean?" Radey's intent has been stifled. He seems genuinely confused.

"You are a living thing, just like me. We both will die. We are in this together. You are simply too afraid to admit it."

"I am afraid of nothing."

"If that is true then look at this house, this house where Cathedra grew up. You know what happened here, don't you? If you are not afraid, then put yourself in her shoes and see what she saw. If you are not afraid of anything then surely you're not afraid of feeling empathy for her."

Radey looks at the house.

"If you cannot do that, then you are a coward," Richard sputters.

A look of curiosity glazes over Radey's eyes. I see in him the faintest trace of emotion. Sadness, perhaps.

And suddenly I am standing behind Richard, gazing outward from Radey's eyes toward my childhood home.

I'm clinging tightly to a shard of broken glass, the one I picked up to defend myself against an imagined monster. It is pressed against Richard's neck and I can't believe it is me pressing it there.

I drop the blade of glass and weep.

Suddenly I remember the day my parents died. I remember how much I loved them. I remember how much it hurt to lose them.

The memory unfurls fully and I fear I may die from the aching in my heart.

Chapter 35

My mother's eyes—those fragile orbs made of the ocean's color—turned so quickly into the eyes of an animal afraid for its own survival.

It's what I remember most, because I'd never seen such terror in a person before, and it made me feel it too.

She stared out into the blinding morning light beyond our dining room window. Because of the sun's glare I couldn't see what she saw from where I sat. And so I was entranced by the sight of her instead. When she finally came out of her stupor and saw how scared I was, she kissed me on the temple to try and keep me calm.

Then she said I had to hide. While lifted in her arms I briefly saw out the window to where she'd been looking. There was a man approaching our house. He was dressed in black and carried a long, large stick which he clung to with both hands while it leaned over his shoulder. The look on his face was grave and empty and I knew we were in trouble the moment I saw him. I remember thinking it was the grim reaper come to get us but I was too scared to say it out loud.

My mother held me so tight I could hardly breathe. She ran in a frenzy from the room. The way her bare feet slapped loudly against the wood floor made my body clench in fear, every step like a gunshot against my ears.

She brought me to a closet beneath the stairs. She opened the closet door and stepped inside. She set me on my feet and kissed me again upon my forehead. She said she was calling the police and everything would be fine. She said to stay hidden no matter what until the police were there. Then she had me sit in the corner of the closet. She piled clothes on top of me until I couldn't see anything and it got hard to breathe.

The closet door shut and everything got real quiet.

Moments would pass with me too terrified to move. I hardly drew breath. I played dead under the clothes like a baby deer in brush.

And then the silence broke with my mother's muffled voice as she argued in another room. I couldn't understand what she said from the muffling but could tell by how loud it was that she was terrified. I understood the sound of fear. I knew the man from outside was in the house with her.

Then I heard a loud thud. And another. Then it got quiet again.

Long, suffocating silence. And darkness like the dark that must've been before the universe existed. I lay helpless in the void. Listening. Waiting for some sign it was safe to leave the closet. I waited until I couldn't bear it and, grim reaper or no grim reaper, I needed to know my mom was okay.

I crept out from the nest of dusty jackets. I pried the closet door open as quietly as I could and took careful, silent steps out into the dull daylight of the house, holding my breath. I traced the path I thought my mother must've taken toward the kitchen and dining room. I walked past the front door of our house. It was hanging open, swaying in the wind. I tiptoed through the kitchen and in the dining room, next to the table I'd been sitting at, I found the man standing and staring out the window, breathing heavily like he'd just been running.

The man was my dad and for a moment—a brief and fleeting moment—I felt safe.

Under the table, near his feet, a motionless body lay slumped. The lifeless body of my mother. I knew she was gone and not just sleeping. Her warmth had disappeared. She was just a thing that couldn't move or do anything anymore. I bumped into the wall behind me. Backing away from the scene carelessly as I was. I let out a squeak.

My dad's eyes darted toward me and when his face honed in on me I saw blood was on it and on his clothes too. "She slipped," he said.

There was nothing behind his eyes that I could recognize. It was like a stranger had put on his body and was controlling him. "But don't worry," he said. "God took her." And then he laughed so loud it made my body jerk. I got so scared my pants got wet with pee. "Same way he's gonna take you." He grinned the way bad guys grin on TV.

He took one step toward me and I became an animal. A fox or deer. No thoughts in my head, just me running. I ran from the room and out the front door. I ran and ran and just kept running.

Down our driveway, near the big tree Mom said Grandpa planted, there were three police cars coming up slowly toward me. I ran as fast as I could to them and all the policemen got out of their vehicles and came to talk to me. One of the officers scooped me up and put me into his car.

They asked me what happened and what was going on. But I couldn't talk. I tried but nothing would come out. I just kept pointing at the house. My eyes wide and scared enough I think they knew something bad had happened and they needed to be careful.

The policeman who put me in his car stayed with me while the others went toward the house. He held me in his arms and told me everything would be okay and that I was safe.

It wasn't long before I heard gunshots and when I tried to look to see what was happening the officer squeezed me tightly and held my face to his chest.

I knew then Dad was dead too and I was all alone but for the stranger holding me in his arms.

Chapter 36

"Cathedra."

One breath.

"Cathedra."

Two.

"Cathedra, you can still help me. There may be a phone—in the house."

I'm trying my best to keep my mind from crumbling, but behind my eyes are bursts of blood like the fists of ghosts pounding, rapid and relentless; my heart a useless clock ticking down until Richard is gone like everything else I've ever loved.

I take a third breath, more slowly this time.

"But you have to go now," he says. "You have to hurry. You have to call an ambulance. Or I will die." His voice is a frail whisper. I can't take my eyes off his skin. Pale in the moonlight, it's the same color as that of every corpse I've ever seen.

"I'm sorry." My voice is an inaudible rasp of air. "I did this to you. I'm so sorry, Richard. I don't know why I did this." The uselessness of words has never been more apparent. Nothing I could say will change anything.

"Go. Now," he says as forcefully as he can muster.

Before I can think of a reason against or for what I am doing the world is whooshing in my ears. I am in a frenzied run toward the house. I am desperate not to lose him.

The universe in all its entirety was born into motion with one explosive, gaseous rupture. That's what my heart feels like, right now. Ruptured.

And the rupture grows when I see the sight before me.

Snaking upward into the sky above the house's rooftop is a long black tendril of smoke. The house is on fire.

And in the time it takes me to try and remember if the fire was my doing, flames have already reached out like arms from every window—yellow and orange incandescent flames lapping outward like the tongues of snakes, feasting on the air around the house.

The fire is a sight of violence in its truest form—blinding and fearsome as the sun—but it doesn't stop my running.

In a blink I'm nearly at the door and already it feels as if I'm in an oven. This must be what it feels like to be a moth, drawn helplessly to a fire.

I reach out my hand toward the door. Once as a child I touched a burning ember, too foolish to know any better. It's the same feeling as I grip the doorknob in my palm. I turn it and push the door open and dark smoke billows outward like ash erupting from a volcano. I push forward into it.

My skin screams in agony; it screams in fear, but the voice of pain is a voice I no longer trust enough to heed so it doesn't stop my mission. All I can see is a blinding murk of rolling gray—smoke unfurling unto smoke—too thick for breath or sight. And behind it pulsing are the house's walls erupting into flame.

I try to think of where a phone would be. I walk blindly until I bump into a counter and realize I must be in the kitchen. I fumble my fingers across the countertop. Every inch of it feels like a lit stove burner.

As I'm reaching through the smoke and fire to find a phone an odd feeling begins to overtake me. It feels like my skin is being stretched, as if my body is a cocoon shrinking in on itself, and for a moment I think I smell someone cooking. And then I realize that's exactly what I smell.

I look down at my body. The black suit I'm wearing is on fire, and with it, so is my skin.

If hell is suffering—unrelenting and absolute, searing and inescapable—then hell is what I am feeling in this moment. Still, there is intent in me untouched by it.

I would rather save Richard than save myself.

With my hands I trace the counter's surface to the wall where I remember a phone once hung, and lo and behold, it still hangs.

The heated plastic of the telephone handset glues to my hand when I lift it from its mounted base. I'm surprised to hear a live dial tone when I place it to my ear. I use my other hand to dial 911. The base's touch-tone buttons feel like melted chocolate as I push them down.

A man with a gravelly voice answers.

"911. What's your emergency?"

I swear the phone is shrinking in my hand, melting from heat.

"Oh god, I don't know where I am. I don't know the address."

"Ma'am, is the phone you're calling from in the same place as your emergency?"

"Yes. Yes, send an ambulance here."

"And will I be able to reach you at this number if I need to?"

The phone is starting to feel like putty in my hand.

"No, I don't think you will."

"And who am I speaking with?"

"I don't know."

"Uhh, well, ma'am. Can you tell me what the nature of your emergency is?"

"A man has been stabbed. I stabbed him. He is bleeding badly and I think he might be dying."

"We're sending an ambulance right away. Now miss, if you could—"

The phone goes dead and the plastic of the handset drips down my hands like melted wax. I drop the now formless glob of plastic and wire to the floor and hope I've done enough.

What happens next is I give up.

I sit down amidst the raging fire and listen to the wood walls as they pop and crackle around me. I breathe the smoke in deeply. The black ash—the breath of death—swirls in my lungs. Pain as I've never felt it before roars in my chest—radiant and excruciating. My lungs close in on themselves. I let out a final scream as the world shows me its worst and I let go of anything I've got left to let go of.

It's not suicide, because none of this is real.

Chapter 37

I wake to the sound of ocean lapping at a distant shore, or perhaps it is the white noise static of a television set. There are human voices in the distance, soft and muffled.

When I open my eyes all I see is white. A white ceiling, and white walls. A soft breath of cool air brushes over me. I'm lying on my back, comfortably, with a window cracked open to my right. Deep, cloudless blue sky beyond it. Somewhere nearby are birds chirping in a gentle song repeated.

Footsteps enter the room but I don't see who they belong to. I continue staring out the window.

"She's awake." It's the voice of an older woman. She's talking to someone outside the room.

"Richard. Is Richard okay?" I ask. My throat is dry and it's hard to speak.

"Yes. Richard will be fine. For now, just get some rest. You were extremely dehydrated and malnourished and we just need to get you healthy again, okay?"

"I was dreaming something wonderful," I say, as if this person is my friend.

"You just relax and get some more sleep." I feel her hand pat gently on my shoulder, to reassure me, to comfort me. She is a kind person.

And I don't argue with her. I close my eyes and let my mind drift.

My gentle breaths rise and fall like a rolling tide.

I feel like I am home.

Mother, I dreamt you held me still.

I was a child, weak and helpless, and you protected me in your arms. I lay beneath your gaze and you nursed me with God's light eternally.

When I woke I was alone.

But the birds outside, and the morning light, and the room I was in...

I felt your presence in them, and it is with me still.

Mother, in my dream you showed me my true self.

This warm, quiet presence within me, and within all things; I knew that it was me, and I was it. And it was you, as well. And everyone else, too.

In the dream we were all one being, inseparable and free, for all eternity.

No longer was there a reason for us to fight and toil against ourselves.

My thoughts roll away like clouds and there is nothing to keep me from sinking into a deep and restful sleep.

Cornelius Corvidae is a singer-songwriter, poet, musician, and birch bark jewelry maker. He wrote *Stranger In The Fire* in 2014. Born in Bemidji, he is based in Minnesota.